KT-582-763

CUPCAKES AND CANDLESTICKS

When Maddy's husband Rob suddenly announces that he's leaving her and moving to Canada with his pretty young employee, her world comes crashing down. As Rob's promises of financial support prove worthless, Maddy finds herself under growing pressure to forge a new life for herself and her four children. She decides to start a catering business, but will it earn enough money — and is that what she really wants? And then she meets the gorgeous Guy in the strangest of circumstances . . .

NORA FOUNTAIN

CUPCAKES AND CANDLESTICKS

Complete and Unabridged

LINFORD
Leicester

First published in Great Britain in 2014

First Linford Edition
published 2015

A catalogue record for this book is available
from the British Library.

ISBN 978–1–4448–2478–0

Published by
F. A. Thorpe (Publishing)
Anstey, Leicestershire

Set by Words & Graphics Ltd.
Anstey, Leicestershire
Printed and bound in Great Britain by
T. J. International Ltd., Padstow, Cornwall

This book is printed on acid-free paper

Prologue

Guy paused at the lychgate. How bleak the cemetery looked with its fine covering of snow. A few flakes of the powdery stuff drifted across his vision, settling on his face before melting away. He'd risen early, unable to sleep and now, though still only six o'clock, there was not another soul in sight.

My darling Isabel — you should be here with me and our wonderful son, warm and alive, not lying under earth frozen solid in this bitter March weather. This is so like the day fourteen years ago when you were taken from me.

His gloved hand stuck briefly to the icy bar as he opened the gate. Inside, he headed for her grave where he disposed of a vase full of dead and dying flowers and replaced them with the dark red roses he brought every year on this sad anniversary.

'I love you, Isabel,' he whispered, sending his words into the ether for the wife he had adored.

As he brushed away some dead grass from the surface of the grave, the creak of the gate alerted him to Dominic's arrival. He stood up and went to greet him, enveloping him in a hug.

'Hello, Dom. You're up early.'

'But not early enough, it seems.'

'Sorry. I should have waited.'

'It's okay, Dad. I know it's something you like to do alone.'

'And I'm sorry, sorry about so many things. This day always reminds me of what I failed to do at the time, so I'm sorry if I was too overwhelmed by my own grief to give you the comfort you needed and deserved as a little five-year-old.'

'You did all right by me, Dad, but we both would have been lost without dear old Mrs Frimley.'

'Yes, she's been more than a housekeeper. Thank goodness she still comes in to help these two helpless males.'

He watched as Dominic lifted his bouquet of pink-tipped yellow roses and inhaled their perfume. With their heady fragrance they had been Isabel's favourite. His own choice of deep red blooms was an expression of his endless love for her. 'Do you want any help?' he asked now.

'No, Dad, thanks. I want to do it myself.'

As he insisted every year. Guy smiled as he remembered Dominic's early efforts, refusing any help. He watched in silence now as his son arranged his roses in another vase.

How utterly helpless he had felt after Isabel's death. All he could do was hold his small son when he cried for his mother, day or night. He wondered now if Dominic had ever heard him sobbing in the night himself, despite efforts to muffle the sound. This was such an emotional day for them both. A tear ran down his cheek.

'Come on, Dad. Big boys don't cry.' They smiled tearfully at each other. 'My turn to do breakfast.'

As they walked home in companionable silence Guy's thoughts went over the long, lonely years without Isabel. Was he to be alone forever? He had tried to fill the void with that disastrous marriage to Vanessa. Now he wondered what had possessed him. She had been young and beautiful and wild, too wild with her vibrant red hair and lissom body. Had she set out to ensnare him? A quiet man, happiest when riding over his Dorset estate with or without Dominic, he had been utterly captivated by her dramatic looks and fun-loving nature. At first. She had been so different and he had been so lonely.

They had met in a pub. He had been there in a conference room, listening to a talk on recent changes in farming and the relevant law. She had come in halfway through with a group of rowdy young farmers. They had been asked to leave, but not before their eyes had met and locked for a few moments.

Instead of leaving the pub after the talk he had glanced into the public bar and there she had been as if waiting for him, her eyes on the door. He gave in to temptation and soon they were having a drink, just the two of them, and arranging to meet again.

He cringed when he remembered the noisy pubs she loved, the karaoke performances in which she was happy to make an exhibition of herself. She tried to persuade him to join in but he drew the line at that. It wasn't his scene. She used to laugh at him, mock him, call him stuffy. By then she had his ring on her finger.

She would fill his house with 'friends' met in pubs and, since cooking wasn't her thing, Mrs Frimley was kept busy cooking for all and sundry and trying to look out for Dominic. Guy's wine cellar was plundered and stocks shrank alarmingly. There was one man he took particular exception to, a sleazy individual of Hispanic origin who was a frequent visitor. Matters came to a head when Guy arrived home from a late business meeting to find her 'friends' in the house and Dominic, then thirteen, giggly from the alcohol she had given him.

No one did that to his son. He roared at them all to get out of his house.

'You coming, babe?' asked Miguel.

'Of course not,' she laughed. 'My husband's home now. You go. I'll see you soon.'

'Not in my house, you won't,' Guy assured her.

'Sorry, Guy darling. It won't happen again.'

'Too right it won't.'

At the time Guy had been debating whether or not to send Dom to his old boarding school. He'd been happy enough there himself. Vanessa's outlandish behaviour made the decision for him. He could never again trust her to look after his son. It was another thing for which he would never forgive her. He would have much preferred to keep Dom at home and attend school as a day boy, but he'd be safer away at boarding school.

Soon afterwards Vanessa took off with her Hispanic friend to sing in a Vegas nightclub, by which time Dominic had settled happily at his school.

Guy put his arm round Dom's shoulders as they walked home. 'While I'm apologising, I'm especially sorry for inflicting Vanessa on you.'

'No need, Dad. She was quite funny at times. Crazy, though, wasn't she?'

'That's one way of putting it. It's put me right off the idea of matrimony, that's for sure.'

'Don't say that, Dad. I won't be here forever and I can't bear to think of you alone for the rest of your life. I'd be very happy for you if you found someone else.'

'No need to worry about me, darling boy. I love it here and if there's a choice I'd rather be here on my own than with another Vanessa. Here we are then. What are we having for breakfast?'

'The full Monty, I think.'

'The full Monty it is.'

Dominic was turning into a very competent cook and was soon putting plates of food on the table.

'Hey, this looks fantastic, Dom. Thank you.'

'My pleasure. Tuck in.'

And as they enjoyed breakfast together Dominic wished with all his heart that his father could find happiness again. He was such a kind, caring man and no one could have a better father. Surely there was some nice woman somewhere who could appreciate his attributes and love him for the man he was.

1

A drift of palest pink caught her eye and Maddy paused, spatula in hand. Outside the window apple blossom was raining like confetti to the orchard floor. Blue tits were pecking away at the birdfeeder, oblivious to Whiskey, their black-and-white cat, lying under a shady mallow. He was watching with half-closed eyes, somnolent, still. Eventually bored, he stood up, slowly stretched to his full height and stalked to the cat flap. After clattering through to the conservatory, he languidly arranged himself on the heated tiles. Maddy returned to her chores.

'What a gorgeous day. It'll be hot later on,' she murmured, slotting bread into the toaster. 'More coffee, Rob?'

Without looking up from the *Times*, Rob held out his cup which Maddy obligingly filled. She felt obliging — a warm, contented, obliging wife and mother. Rob flicked the paper and turned the page. His eyes locked with Maddy's for a second and her smile faded. His expression was strange, distant — almost hostile.

The piano in the dining room fell silent. 'Thank God for that! She'll never make grade six!' he declared scathingly.

'Oh, I don't know. Sophie's very musical — both twins are. They're brilliant on the violin, too. You're very crotchety this morning, darling.'

'Is it too much to ask for a bit of peace and quiet while I eat my breakfast?'

'Impossible, I'd say, with four teenagers around. Another six years and they may all be gone, and then we'll be rattling around in this big house, wondering what on earth to do with ourselves.'

Sophie poked her head round the door. 'Mummy, did you iron our tennis things?' she asked.

'They're in your wardrobe, love.'

'Ace!'

'Can't you and Dawn iron your own things? You're nearly fifteen, for God's sake!'

'Daddy! We're far too busy,' Sophie informed him, pulling a 'who's rattled his cage?' face at Maddy.

'And your mother's not, I suppose?'

Sophie sighed dramatically. '*You* don't iron your own shirts.'

'Sophie!' Maddy was shocked by this rudeness from the most complacent of the twins.

'I do quite enough footing the bills to keep this place going.'

'It's a very nice place and we do appreciate it,' Maddy assured him.

It was indeed — a large family house in Bournemouth within a mile of the sea, with five bedrooms, three bathrooms and a couple of en-suites. Like the other properties in the tree-lined road, it had almost an acre of garden. Unfortunately these properties were now regarded as prime sites for greedy developers, and Maddy was appalled at the speed with which a house could be put on the market, sold, demolished, and replaced by a millionaire's mansion or block of flats. Not that theirs would suffer that fate. It suited them ideally.

Could Rob be worried about money? Maddy wondered. Something was wrong, that much was clear. But surely the estate agency he and Simon ran was thriving? The property market was tailing off in general, she knew that, but it was still fairly buoyant at the luxury end of the market, where the agency specialised.

'Dawn!' Sophie yelled up to her twin, unaware of Maddy's concern. 'They're in the wardrobe. Can you bring mine down, too?'

'Sit down and have some breakfast,' Maddy urged. 'Do you fancy an egg, or some bacon?'

'Do you want us to get fat?'

'Too late!' said Hugo. His tall, loose-limbed body filled the doorway, a teasing grin on his handsome young face. 'I fancy bacon, egg and anything else that's going, if that's okay, Mum.'

'Of course it is.'

'Pig!' muttered Sophie.

'I'm a growing boy. We men don't finish growing till we're at least eighteen — another year to go.'

'Hmph!' came from behind the newspaper.

'We'll just have grapefruit and toast,' Sophie announced.

'And dear little Dawn can't speak for herself?' Hugo taunted gently, helping himself to orange juice.

'She's minutes younger than I am, and trusts in my exquisite good taste!'

Maddy smiled at their familiar banter and broke another egg into the pan.

A heavy clumping down the stairs heralded the arrival of Jamie, at twelve the youngest. 'Mum, I forgot to put my football kit in the wash,' he said. 'Can you give me a sick note?'

Maddy cringed, waiting for the explosion. She didn't have long to wait. The paper lowered.

'You're having no more sick notes.

13

You can damn well wear the kit as it is, if you can't be bothered to get organised.'

Jamie's eyes pleaded with Maddy but she sighed and turned away. Now was not the time to cross his father.

'Breakfast, Jamie.'

Rob came from behind his paper to watch his younger son fill a bowl with chocolate-coated cereal. 'That's disgusting!' he said.

A quarter of an hour later Jamie slammed out, complete with soiled football kit, to catch the minibus to his prep school. The twins, giggling about the first double lesson with the French master they had a crush on, departed in high spirits for their exclusive girls' school.

'Can you give me a lift, Dad?' asked Hugo, whose school was in the same direction as Rob's agency.

'No, I can't! For God's sake, what did you want that fancy bike for?'

'Not for carrying a ton of books and a tennis racket.'

14

'I'll drop you off, love,' Maddy volunteered. 'I'm going to Waitrose this morning.'

'No!' Rob barked and they both stared at him. 'I have to talk to you, Maddy.'

'Can't we talk this evening?'

'I need to talk to you now, before I go. Alone,' he tacked on.

She shrugged apologetically. 'Sorry, Hugo. Can you manage?'

Pulling a face behind his father's back, he slung his haversack onto his back and let himself out of the back door.

'You were a bit harsh on him,' Maddy said gently.

'You baby the lot of them.'

Rob had been increasingly snappy lately. She'd begun to wonder if he had a health problem, assuming the business was all right.

'What did you want to talk about?'

'There's no easy way to say this.' Oh God, there was something wrong. Maddy steeled herself for the worst.

They'd been through bad times before. *For richer, for poorer* . . . The agency was ticking over during the latest recession. It wasn't as hard-hit as those dealing with the lower end of the market. *In sickness and in health* . . . She would help him through it, whatever it was.

'I'm leaving you, Maddy.'

Maddy was still summoning her most heroic response when she realised what he'd said.

'You're — what?'

Rob looked down and mumbled, 'You heard. I'm leaving.'

'But . . . why? I mean, last night, you made . . . ' It couldn't be. A whirlwind had picked up her world, twirled it round and hurled it back in a jagged heap. She checked herself before shrieking, 'You screwed me last night, for God's sake!'

'I thought you wanted it.'

'You thought *I* wanted it? You mean you were being accommodating?'

'Well, no, of course not.'

16

'You should have told me it was your parting shot!'

'No need to be crude. I could have left first and then told you.'

'So you're doing the decent thing! Well, I'm surprised you didn't just leave. Why, Rob? Why are you leaving? Where are you going? And what will you tell the children?'

He had the grace to look shame-faced. 'I thought it best if you told them.'

'I see.' Cowardly, too. 'And when's all this going to happen?'

'I'm leaving today.'

Maddy, usually so calm, tried to still her shaking hands. 'Rob, tell me this is a joke. You can't abandon us. Why would you want to?'

'You're too wrapped up in the kids to notice anything wrong. I'm a long way down your list of priorities.'

'That's not fair. Of course they *need* me, and there *are* four of them. That's a lot of need, but they need you, too. When did you last go to a school function, or take them out for the day?'

'With such a super-efficient mother, they don't need me for anything, except to pay the bills.'

'So you're walking out because I'm too efficient. That doesn't make sense. You're just shifting the blame onto me, when I've done nothing to deserve it. You sound as if you hate me.'

'I don't hate you, but you must admit we've lost touch with each other. You take no interest at all in the business that brings in the money.'

'And whose fault is that? You always say you want to relax and forget about work once you're home. Not that you've been home much lately. You've been spending more and more time at the office. My God!' A nasty thought occurred to her. 'You've got someone else!'

A whole lot of incidents rushed to mind. Those evenings when she'd phoned him to find out what time he'd be home, so that the steaks would be just right, or when friends had been invited round and he might need a reminder, or she wanted him to pick up some wine. He always had a plausible excuse. He was working late or showing a property to a potential client. Sometimes the background noise didn't match the excuse. Sometimes an empty property sounded more like a busy restaurant or bar. She'd always believed him, or given him the benefit of the doubt, poor trusting fool that she'd been.

'Yes,' he admitted, having the grace to look ashamed. 'I've been trying to tell you for weeks. I didn't want to hurt you but yes, there is someone. Holly and I have fallen for each other.'

'Holly, as in the glossy, confident bitch who came to dinner at that restaurant with Simon and the other couple? The Canadian girl you took on a few months ago?'

Holly, dark and vivacious, flirting madly with all three men at the table.

'I know how it must look. At that time we were trying to fight the attraction but from the moment she walked into the office for an interview, it was like, well . . . ' He shrugged, a sheepish smile tugging at his mouth.

'A *coup de foudre?*' she suggested bitterly.

'I guess so. We tried to deny it, we really did, but . . . '

'Spare me the clichés. I can see now why you used to come home psyched up for sex,' she remembered bitterly. 'And then suddenly — pouf! You were always too tired. That must be when *she* took over.'

She. Holly. The slick, dark-haired Canadian, her sleek, geometric bob swinging in a curtain to just below her ears. Holly of the heart-shaped, perfectly made-up face, pouting mouth and long-lashed dark eyes.

Maddy caught a glimpse of herself in the small mirror on the wall beside the Aga. Her shoulder-length hair, blonde and wavy, was drying on its own, as usual. She was too busy serving up breakfast and helping everyone else to

20

start their day to bother with her appearance. Her face, with its neat, unremarkable features, was free of make-up, her dry forty-six-year-old skin revealing a few tiny wrinkles, her cheeks glowing but only from the heat of the Aga.

No contest, really, if that woman had set out to steal her husband. But what about love, and all those vows they'd taken eighteen years ago?

'I love you, Rob,' she reminded him, simply and unemotionally.

She shivered in the warm kitchen, aware of the shabby T-shirt and jeans under her pinafore. Bereft in advance of his departure, she tried to think of something, anything, which might change his mind. Nothing would come. Rob had become a stranger.

'I'm sorry. I'll make the house over to you.'

'And the mortgage?' she queried drily.

'Paid off.'

'Since when?'

He shifted uncomfortably. 'Since last week. I'll pay a lump sum into your bank, too. Simon's buying me out at the agency.'

'You're leaving the agency, too?'

He couldn't meet her eyes. 'We're going to Canada, to Montreal where Holly comes from.'

'So we'll never see you again?'

'No need to be melodramatic! It's only hours away. Once we're settled, the kids can come and spend holidays with us.'

'I don't want them spending their holidays with 'us' — not when the 'us' means you and her! I can't bear it. Don't do this to us, please, Rob. This is a bad dream. Please, for the children's sake . . . '

'The children are already doing their own thing. Hugo will be off to university next year. The twins will follow a couple of years later. That's if they buckle down to some work, and stop treating life as one big social whirl.'

'They *do* work. What's wrong with

having fun, too? And Jamie? What about Jamie? He's only twelve. He worships you.' And he was in the painful throes of puberty.

'Don't be absurd. He rarely talks to me.'

'He rarely gets the chance!'

Poor Jamie. He was always asking if Dad would be going to football matches or swimming competitions. All his efforts were for Rob, who had excelled at sport in his youth. And Jamie often needed help with his science homework. Not Maddy's strong point. It *was* Rob's, though.

'Jamie's a spoilt brat. He'll survive.'

Maddy saw red. Jamie had never had Hugo's strengths, nor the twins' independence. 'Don't you ever call him that! The boy idolises you, you fool! If you're going to leave, just go. We'll manage.'

She had hateful visions of abandoning this tree-lined street in an up-market area of Bournemouth and trading down to some characterless

23

semi in a far-from-salubrious area, getting rid of the people-carrier that accommodated all of them and their possessions, leaving their friends . . .

'Maddy, I'm truly sorry. I know this will cause some disruption, but it would be dishonest of me to stay and pretend to be happy when I want to be somewhere else, with someone else. It'll be for the best for all of us, in the long run.' He stood up and hovered, as if he suddenly didn't know what to do with his hands. 'I'll go and finish packing.'

'I wasn't aware you'd started!'

Instinct took her to his study where the Antler cases she'd given him for his last birthday were lined up. He'd made a unilateral decision and nothing she could say would change his mind.

'You bastard! You absolute, total bastard!'

She said it almost to herself. She wouldn't cry, she wouldn't give him that satisfaction. What would they do, though, she and the children? She listened to drawers and doors being flung open; imagined his final, speedy packing. The next moment, he was coming downstairs with the last of his luggage.

'What did I do wrong?' she asked quietly.

'Nothing. It was nothing you did, Maddy. I just fell for Holly hook, line and sinker. We're crazy about each other.' Maddy felt a stabbing sensation in the region of her solar plexus. 'It became something we couldn't ignore.' The knife twisted. 'I won't be ungenerous but, if things get tough, we do live in a welfare state.'

'I can't believe you said that. After all your pontifications about people sponging off the state. Go away, Rob. You've become a monster. I don't know you anymore. Just go away.'

'I'm going.'

He couldn't sweep out dramatically. It took three journeys to get his luggage to the car. Then she listened to the heavy clunk of his Mercedes, the gentle vroom of the engine, the crunch on gravel, and then . . . nothing.

Maddy sank onto the bottom stair, her head in her hands. Later she would cry. Right now, she was too numb.

This was the end of a chapter, but the beginning of . . . what? Facing life alone. Bringing up the children alone. Paying household bills, school fees for the boys, car expenses. The daily help, Val.

Who was now letting herself in through the back door to the utility room.

'Morning, Maddy!' she called cheerfully. 'How are we today, then?' She came bustling through into the hall and stopped dead. 'Why, what on earth's the matter?'

Maddy stood up slowly. 'Let's have a cup of coffee, Val.' She led the way to the kitchen.

'You sit down, Maddy, and tell me what's up.'

'No, really, I'd rather keep busy.' She set about making coffee while Val loaded the dishwasher with the breakfast things.

'Thing is, Val . . . well . . . I may have to let you go.'

That was not what she'd intended to say at all.

Val's face dropped. She always insisted she didn't need the money; she just loved coming there. Her husband, Reg, might be happy to spend his retirement sitting around reading or growing things in his allotment, but Val liked to be busy. She did voluntary work at the hospital, learned Spanish at evening class and had just joined a gym.

'Let me go? Are you sacking me? I thought you found me helpful. I can't believe it.'

'Oh God! I put that badly. I'm sorry, Val. You're more than helpful. I've come to regard you as a friend, but Rob's . . . '

'He's gone, hasn't he?'

Maddy nodded, pinching her lips together to check the urge to cry. It was no good. Her face puckered and the tears fell.

'He's gone off with that flighty bit

that works for him, I suppose. That skinny madam from the States.'

'Canada,' Maddy corrected absently. The assertion brought her up short. 'How did you know, Val?'

'I've heard the gossip. Didn't believe it at first, though I did see them a time or two in his car in town. No man in his right mind would prefer her to you. You'll need a solicitor, love. He can't up and leave you penniless, with four teenagers to support.' She shook her neat, blonde-rinsed head. 'He must be mad. I hear Tony Maitland from Southbourne way is good. He's done one or two divorces that I know of. Don't worry about me, though; I'll carry on as usual and you can pay me as and when.'

'I can't let you work for nothing!'

'I enjoy coming here. You know I do. It gets me out of the house — well, flat. Gets me away from his nibs. Always under my feet since he retired.'

The house looked extra spick and span by the time Val left. Maddy had spent the morning going through the household accounts and trying to make some decisions. She would certainly need to consult a solicitor. She ought to consider finding a job, too. But doing what? She had given up her job as an air stewardess when she married Rob.

He may have promised to look after her financially but he had also promised to love, honour, cherish, etc., till death us do part. And look where that had got her!

It was a daunting prospect, having to earn a living after all these years of being a wife and mother. She hadn't a clue where to start. She and Rob had met at the wedding of mutual friends. They had married a few months later and she'd become pregnant with Hugo within three months. She had felt lucky at the time, not having to work, considering the problems some of her friends had had in finding adequate child care. Now she realised she had given up her career-building years and was on the bottom rung again.

So what now? She'd have to train as — something or other.

She'd better start by talking to their solicitor. Old Cedric Robinson was a bit of a fuddy-duddy but he'd dealt with their affairs for years.

He agreed to see her that day.

'I must say I'm surprised you chose to contact me,' he said in a flat tone.

The office was in a time warp. Despite the smell of polish, flecks of dust floated thickly in a shaft of light.

'Why do you say that? You've always been our solicitor. I thought you'd be the best person to tell me how I stand.'

'But this is a domestic matter.'

'Quite.'

'And naturally I shall be acting for your husband.'

'Acting . . . ?'

'He's asked me to deal with . . . everything.'

'Meaning?'

'I see no need for secrecy. You'll find out soon enough. There's the sale of his share in the agency, which is well under way.'

'He did tell me he was selling out.'

'And the divorce.'

'Divorce? Oh! Oh, my God! That makes it so final. I didn't realise there was any urgency.'

'There's no point in hanging around. My best advice to you is to instruct a solicitor of your own.' Like that Tony Someone-or-other Val had suggested. 'I shouldn't be saying this but I'm truly sorry this has happened. Make sure you get your fair share, preferably before Rob goes off to Canada.'

'Are you suggesting he'll try and leave us penniless?'

'Well, as I said, I can't advise you. I know he was planning to make the house over to you, but what will you live on? You must protect your inter-ests.'

'I'm sure he'll look after us. He said as much.'

'Yes, well, I'm afraid fine feelings go out of the window after marital break-up. In the end, marriage boils down to property, money. Don't forget the third party involved. She'll be putting pressure on him to get the best deal.'

Maddy shook her head, suddenly feeling sick. This didn't sound like the Rob she had known and loved for so long. Perhaps he was going through the male menopause. Didn't that happen in the forties? Rob was forty-nine, three years older than Maddy. He was probably flattered that someone as young and glamorous as Holly, still in her twenties, should fancy him. He had always liked the fact that Maddy was a bit younger than himself, and in many ways looked up to him. Now, she felt old. Holly had youth and looks and work experience on her side.

'It's all pretty depressing, isn't it?'

Cedric Robinson looked at his watch.

'I'm sorry, Maddy, but I have another appointment. I fitted you in out of courtesy. I really have to go now. Bear in mind what I've said, though.'

32

Oh, she would. She did. As she drove home, she felt something entirely alien to her nature: a fierce, almost over-whelming hatred. Not towards Rob, though. He was clearly weak, besotted by the youthful, glamorous Holly. It was towards Holly herself she felt that hatred. How *dare* she! She knew he had a family. She had even met one or two of the children, who popped in at the agency occasionally for various reasons. How bloody *dare* she!

And why had Rob said, not that long ago, that he thought his partner, Simon, was getting it together with Holly? That hadn't surprised her at the time. Simon played the field. A twice-divorced man with no children, he had a perfect right to do so. When had Holly decided to withdraw her favours from Simon and turn her charm on Rob? Or had it been a smokescreen to conceal the truth from Maddy?

Once home, she prepared a lamb casserole and put it in the oven. Comfort food to warm and cheer.

Jamie was home first, hair dishevelled, face streaked with mud.

'We won!' he announced, dropping his sports bag to the kitchen floor. A big grin lit his dark eyes, so heart-breakingly like his father's.

'Well done, darling.' Later she would be the one to wipe that smile from his face. Her hatred extended to Rob. Jamie scowled more often than he smiled these days. 'I'll get you a drink and some cake while you empty that lot into the laundry basket in the utility room.'

The scowl threatened but retreated. 'Okay, Mum. Any of your seedcake left?'

'There is, unless Hugo was at it in the night. No, here we are.' She took the remaining third of the cake out of the tin and cut him a generous slice. 'Like some milk with that?'

'Thanks, Mum.'

The twins were next. They burst in,

34

chattering and laughing. 'Hi, Mum. Hi, Jamie,' they said in unison on their way through the kitchen.

After depositing their dirty tennis gear in the utility room they were back, still carrying on an almost exclusive conversation. 'Do you want tea?' Dawn asked her twin.

'Yeah, great! And some of that cake.'

'You're not going to finish it up, are you?' asked Jamie.

'Might do,' Sophie teased. 'No, course not — don't want to get fat and spotty!'

'Tea for you, Mum?'

'Thanks, Dawn. That'd be great.'

They were in such a good mood. Why did Maddy have to be the one to break their hearts? At that moment, her hatred towards Rob became incandescent. She had to fight hard to contain it.

'Something smells great. What's for tea?' asked Dawn.

'Lamb casserole.'

'Mm! Our favourite. What time will

Hugo be home?'

'He's got games till — ' She consulted the wall-clock. ' — about now.'

'And will Dad be home for tea?'

'No, not tonight, love.'

Maddy caught the glance the twins exchanged and wondered . . .

★ ★ ★

'Fruit salad and cream, anyone?' Maddy asked as the girls collected the plates.

'No cream for us,' Sophie replied.

'I think I will,' said Dawn, to everyone's surprise.

'Oh go on, then, I will too.'

Hugo rolled his eyes. 'I certainly will. How about you, Jamie?'

'I don't know where you put it,' Maddy laughed, considering the enormous plates of meat and vegetables they had both polished off.

'We're growing boys, aren't we, Jamie?' Hugo said, winking at his younger brother.

Why did they all have to be so cheerful? How could she spoil the mood?

Bowls of fruit salad and cream were duly consumed.

'Bags first on the piano,' said Dawn, standing to collect the fruit bowls.

'Leave that,' Maddy ordered, a trifle sharply in her nervousness.

'What is it, Mum?' Hugo asked curiously.

'Sit down, Dawn,' Maddy told her more gently.

'Is this something to do with Dad wanting to talk to you alone this morning?' asked Hugo.

'Yes, it is.'

'Where is Dad?' asked Jamie.

'He never eats with us these days,' said Dawn, with a meaningful glance at Sophie.

Maddy wondered how many 'meaningful glances' between the twins she had missed. Clearly they'd realised things had been different for a while.

He always used to eat with them in the evenings. It was ages since that had happened. There had been so many people to show round properties after hours, so many conferences — mostly invented, she realised now.

'Your father won't be eating with us again.' Maddy twisted the edge of the tablecloth in her fingers, adding, before they assumed his demise, 'He's left us, I'm afraid.'

No half-truths. Teenagers always cut to the chase.

'I'm not staying, then. I'll go and live with him.'

'I'm sorry, Jamie, love. That's not an option. Your father's going to live in Canada.'

'I want to go with him.'

'Don't you understand, squirt?' said Hugo. 'He's going off with that tart he works with. That's it, isn't it, Mum?'

'Oh, gross!' said Dawn.

So they all knew or had had an inkling!

'Is it true, Mummy?' asked Sophie.

38

'I'm afraid so, sweetheart.'

'But what are we going to do?'

She looked round at their dear faces, so precious to her. Why not to their father? How could he do this? The boys were scowling. The girls looked worried.

'Good question,' said Hugo. 'Like, what are we supposed to live on?'

'How could he do it?' demanded Dawn. 'We're not that dreadful, are we?'

'You're not dreadful at all, love. It isn't your fault. I don't even think it's my fault. As to what we're to live on, well, I haven't worked it out just yet. But we'll survive, of that I'm sure.'

'We'll have no money,' said Dawn. 'We'll all have to go out to work.'

'I shall leave school,' declared Hugo. 'We don't need him. I don't ever want to see him again. He's been so horrible recently and now we know why. He's a total shit! I hate him!'

Maddy put her hand over Hugo's. He was on the verge of tears. 'You have to finish your exams, darling. Your school is expensive, it's true, but this term's paid for, as is Jamie's. How about a sixth-form college for the final year?'

'What about me? I'm not going to a state school!' Jamie cried in horror.

'They're very good in Bournemouth,' Maddy assured him.

'I don't care! I'm going to Hugo's school after this term. I'll write to Dad.'

'Shall we have to give up music? And school trips?' asked Sophie.

'Shall we have to get free meal tickets?' Dawn asked in horror. 'Like some of the scholarship kids?'

'I thought that was done discreetly?'

'Oh, it is, but everyone knows who gets them.'

'Oh dear! Well, we're not penniless yet. Your father's paid off the mortgage and is putting some money in my bank account to tide us over until it's all sorted out.'

'What do you mean?' asked Hugo. 'You're going to divorce him, I suppose.'

'It's what he wants.'

'Don't give him what he wants, then he can't marry that bitch!'

'Dear Hugo, there's not much point in refusing him, is there?'

'Come on, Sophie. Let's play some duets.'

Which the twins proceeded to do, loudly and aggressively.

'How about you, Jamie? What homework have you got?'

'Maths,' he growled.

'Your best thing, eh?'

'If you want any help with homework, tonight or any other time, I'll help,' Hugo offered generously.

Maddy smiled at him. He was such a delight, clever and kind — what a combination. He might well be her rock in weeks to come. She squeezed his shoulder before gathering the remaining dishes from the table.

'Thanks, Hugo.'

'We'll talk later.'

'Tomorrow, after I've made some enquiries.'

'Tomorrow.'

2

'Mum, are you awake?'

Yes, but I don't want to be. Maddy had been awake most of the night, turning over various options and coming up with zilch.

'I've brought you a cup of tea, Mum.'

She sat up wearily. 'That's kind of you, Hugo.'

'I haven't slept too well, actually. I've been thinking.'

'You, too.' She sipped her tea, weak but well brewed, just as she liked it. 'Perfect. What have you been thinking, then?'

'About how we're going to cope, what we could do. I could leave school, for a start, and get a job.'

'Absolutely not.'

'Well then, I'll get a Saturday job, stacking shelves or something.'

'That's not a bad idea, provided it

doesn't interfere with your schoolwork. It'd give you some pocket money.'

'Not much help to you, though.'

'My problems are just that, Hugo — mine, and I'll be the one to solve them.'

'Oh, Mum.'

'Got to be positive. As people say, this is the first day of the rest of your life.' He reached to hug her. 'Watch out for my tea!' she laughed. 'Listen, I've been making mental lists. I'm going to see a solicitor. One of my own. Old Cedric wasn't a lot of help. Not his fault; he can't work for husband and wife when divorce is on the horizon.'

'He's a bit past it anyway, isn't he?'

Maddy laughed. 'He is getting on a bit. I'll have to see the bank manager, too. I wonder if he'll tell me to go elsewhere? The main thing is to find out how we stand, what to do if we become destitute, and how I could earn a living. Incidentally, I've got one or two ideas about that.'

'That sounds positive.'

'Can't afford not to be.' She set down her empty cup. 'I'd better get the others up. Thanks for the tea, Hugo, and the support.'

* * *

When all the children had left for school, she phoned the bank. 'Hi, Tara.' Maddy would recognise that smoky voice anywhere. 'Can I have a word with Richard?' Their bank manager, Richard Holmes, had become a friend over the years.

'Hang on a moment.' She kept her waiting for what seemed like ages. 'He's rather tied up at the moment. Could you come in later?'

'Okay. What time?'

'Elevenish?'

'Fine. Can you tell me how much is in my current account?'

'I'll have to identify you first.'

Maddy laughed. 'Don't be ridiculous, Tara.'

'Sorry. It's a bit tricky, Mrs. Leighton.'

'What is? Oh, look, forget it. I'll just see Richard later.'

Was this how she would be treated from now on, now that she had no visible means of support? Rob had promised to pay a lump sum into the bank, but it didn't sound like it was very much. Nor did she know if there would be any further sums. If not, how long would it last? Around three months, she reckoned. She'd never felt more insecure.

She hung up, disgruntled. No, not disgruntled. Furious! It appeared that her only identity to date, since the day she gave up work, had been 'wife of' and 'mother of'. Whatever happened in the future, she was determined to become a person in her own right — the person she would have been, had she not agreed to marry Rob and give up work all those years ago. Now she had to embark on a new career in her mid-forties.

Leaving the house tidy, she drove to the bank. There she informed a clerk who appeared to be at a loose end that she had an appointment. The clerk disappeared into an inner sanctum. As the waiting time dragged on she imagined them discussing her. Seeing a stand packed with leaflets, she went over and grabbed a handful.

'Mr Holmes will see you now, Mrs. Leighton.'

'Thank you.'

The manager's door closed. 'Take a seat, Maddy.'

'You know what's happened, I suppose?'

'Rob has been to see me. I'm really sorry, Maddy. He said he was prepared to support you and the children, but I have to say he sounded a bit shifty about it. I've seen this kind of situation before and, as Rob's leaving the country, I'd advise you not to hold your breath.'

'What, then? And how much is in my account? Tara couldn't tell me.'

'Sorry, she had instructions not to. Here's your latest balance.'

Maddy scrutinised the slip of paper. 'And that's Rob's lump sum?'

'It is.'

'Not a lot, is it?'

'No. If I were you, I'd check the benefits you're entitled to, if push comes to shove. How about work? What kind of work have you done in the past?'

'I was an air stewardess when we met. What a cliché — we met on a plane, except that we didn't; we met at a wedding. Rob insisted I give up work when we got married.'

'I see. Well, it does seem to be a young person's job — no disrespect intended. It's just not the thing to return to once you've had years out bringing up a family, and with the family still needing you.'

'I agree.'

'Perhaps you could consider some kind of training.'

'Training's a good idea. Surviving

while training could be difficult. As to benefits, well I've thought about it, but I really don't want to go down that road.'

'You may have to, for a time. Go and talk to the bods at the town hall.' He gestured towards the leaflets she had put on the table. 'Are you considering starting a business?'

Starting your own business, the top leaflet was headed. She laughed. 'Not really. I'm keeping an open mind. I wanted something to read while I waited. I mean, what sort of business could I run?'

'You could capitalise on your skills. I've got one customer who runs an ironing agency, another who has a team of cleaning ladies. With so many women going out to work, domestic skills are at a premium. Not everyone wants, or can afford, live-in help.'

'I'll give it some thought.'

* * *

Once the money in the bank had run out, the long-term future would be uncertain. Maddy fought back the hatred, the misery, the solitude, and concentrated on the practical.

Training was the next thing to consider. She rather fancied the idea of running a business. After all, it couldn't be so very different from running a home. She could do something connected with food or horticulture, maybe, but she hadn't a clue about starting up, keeping accounts or anything.

Perhaps a qualification would help. She donned jeans and a sweatshirt and drove up to the university to see what was on offer. She could have phoned first, but she wouldn't know who to ask for or where to start.

The careers department couldn't have been more helpful. 'You could do a degree in three years full-time, or five years part-time,' said Mike, one of the advisers.

'And live on what?' She explained her circumstances.

'Yes, I see. That could be a problem. Look.' He consulted his watch. 'Let's discuss this over a drink in the union bar. It's my lunchtime.'

'Oh, I couldn't take up your spare time,' she protested.

'My pleasure.'

She expected to stick out like a sore thumb among young students. While Mike joined the crowd pressed against the bar, though, she found the students at her table more than willing to chat. There were quite a few people in the bar around her age, too, probably lecturers.

'Here we are, then.'

'You know, I don't think I could spend the next three or five years studying for a degree. I'd rather like to do something practical like run a business, starting fairly soon, but God knows what kind. I hardly think I'd fit in here. They're all kids, the students. They're not much older than my oldest son.'

'See that table over there?' By now

there were eight or nine in eager discussion around it.

'The lecturers, you mean?'

He laughed. 'They're all students, mature students, except the young blonde woman — she's a history lecturer.'

'Really? What a topsy-turvy world.'

'Tell you what — we can grab a sandwich in the canteen and then I'll give you some bumph on the courses on offer. You can take it home and study it.'

'Thanks. I didn't realise there was such an interesting place right here on my doorstep.'

* * *

The prospect of a new environment and being surrounded by lively young and not-so-young students was both exhilarating and exhausting. Maddy went home to change into a smart suit with a crisp blouse and modest heels. She felt like going to bed for a couple of hours but she might as well do the benefit thing. Town Hall, Richard had said.

Someone directed her to a large room. Rows of seats in the centre were occupied by those she had always considered the hopeless, the hapless, the work-shy. Now she was one of them, and her perspective would have to change.

The suit was a mistake, she realised from the inquisitive glances she was getting. She shouldn't have bothered. Everyone else was in black or dark colours, mostly shabby jeans and T-shirts, with trainers. She hadn't realised there was a uniform for the dole queue. A number was called and a man in his twenties stood up and ambled over to a desk, where he spoke to an interviewer through a glass screen. He answered some questions, signed a form and ambled back, stopping to address the man on the end of the row.

'Will you be long, Dave?' he asked quietly.

'Depends on this shower, don't it?'

'There's work down at the site. I'll wait in the van.'

'Cheers, Nige.'

Benefit fraud, right under her nose.

Maddy was about to concede that coming here was a mistake when she spotted a sign that said 'Enquiries'.

That was what she needed. She joined the short queue. It was a bit like Argos, really, except that you didn't get some nice new purchase at the end of it. At last it was her turn. By now she was dying for a cup of tea and regretted not bringing her usual bottle of water. She hadn't expected to be here so long.

'How can I help?'

Maddy found herself looking through the safety screen into a humourless face with sharp grey eyes behind metal-framed glasses. John Henderson, said the nameplate on his desk. He looked pretty unpleasant, but he couldn't bite. He was a civil servant, so he could jolly well serve and be civil about it.

'I'd like to know what benefits I'd be

entitled to if I became penniless.'

'What kind of question is that? Have you got your P45?' What the hell was that? 'Have you lost your job?'

'No, I've lost my husband.'

'Children?'

'No, I've still got the children, all four of them.'

'With you?'

'Not physically but yes, they live with me.'

'Have you been in touch with the child support agency?'

'Er — look, I came here to get some answers, yet you seem to be asking all the questions.'

'You can't just walk in here and collect benefits.' Really? That was exactly what she thought people did. 'Fill in this form and take a ticket from the machine. You'll be called when it's your turn.'

She glanced from the long form to the ticket machine. *Just like the deli counter*, she joked to herself. She turned back to him. 'Haven't you got any leaflets setting out the benefits on offer?'

'We consider each case separately.'

'So you haven't got any information on the actual benefits?'

'Look, lady, you can't come in here — ' He looked her up and down, assessing the cost of her outfit. ' — and expect special treatment. Just fill in the form and we can arrange for someone to come out and visit you.'

'At home?'

His eyes narrowed with suspicion. She became aware of the look of horror on her face at the thought of someone like him invading her private space, her home, looking round, asking questions, contaminating the place. She filled in the form as best she could and slid it back.

'Nice address,' he commented with a malicious smirk.

'We like it.'

'I'm sure you do. Right, well, we'll process this and get in touch.'

'When is that likely to be?'

'Why? Are you planning to go away?'

Maddy realised now why they needed safety screens. She stood up intending to push back her chair with sufficient force to indicate her fury but, unfortunately, it was bolted to the floor. Her frustrated anger showed in her stiff-backed march to the exit.

Damn! The kids would soon be home and she hadn't given a thought to dinner. A slight detour brought her to Tesco's car park, where she threw the makings of a meal into a trolley plus a few treats and snacks for her abandoned offspring.

Which was just as well because, as she let herself in, she found Jamie and the twins raiding the fridge for what they described as ready consumables.

'We're having a cup of tea, Mum,' Dawn informed her. 'Would you like one?'

'Wouldn't I just!' Maddy hugged her in gratitude. 'After I've put some of this stuff away.'

'I'll help,' Sophie offered. 'Mm,

looks like we're having chicken with stir-fried vegetables and couscous.' Maddy nodded. 'I'll leave some of this out then.'

Maddy sank wearily onto a chair, thankfully accepting a cuppa. 'Good day?' she asked her unusually quiet younger son.

Jamie was sitting opposite with a glass of milk, a portion of cold bread-and-butter pudding he'd found in the fridge, and a banana. He glanced up from under a troubled brow and quickly down again. 'It was okay.'

'How was games?'

'I didn't play. I told them I felt sick.'

'And did you?'

'Not really.'

Maddy darted a look at the twins. Normally they would react to this by teasing but today they looked concerned.

'What, then?'

'What's the point of trying for the school team if I've got to leave?'

'We don't know that yet.'

'Well, I need to know.'

'Darling, just carry on for now as if nothing's changed. Your fees are paid to the end of the summer term. By then, I should have some idea of what we're going to do. I didn't ask for this situation any more than you did.'

'I know, but that doesn't help.'

Which, thankfully, was when Hugo wafted in like a breath of fresh air, blond hair windswept, cheeks flushed, eyes bright from the bike ride home. Maddy felt a rush of love for her firstborn. He was so handsome, so cheerful, so uncomplicated — until now, at least.

He quickly took in the concern on Maddy's face, and the truculent obstinacy on Jamie's. 'Trouble, half-pint?' he asked, ruffling Jamie's hair.

'We're off to do homework and piano practice,' Sophie announced.

'Make sure you both wash your hands after eating those buttery teacakes,' Maddy reminded them, unable to comprehend why, from the moment they arrived home from school, they all needed to 'graze'. She was quite sure she used to have to wait till supper was ready.

'Will do.' The door closed with a swish behind them.

Hugo poured himself some tea and sat down opposite his younger brother. 'Look, I know it's hard, Jamie, but it's worse for Mum.'

'How is it?'

'Well, I suppose she's got to be Mum and Dad from now on. She's got to run the home and somehow bring in some dosh.'

'Oh, yeah, and how's she going to do that?'

Maddy seared the chicken breasts, then left them to cook slowly with the lid on and joined them at the table. 'I haven't worked it out yet, Jamie, but I've been looking into it. I might train as something or other. Richard, our bank manager, suggested that, but I'm not so sure. I called at the university and picked up this pile of leaflets to see what's on offer.'

'You have been busy!' Hugo exclaimed, thumbing through the leaflets. 'Never thought of you as a career woman.'

She didn't mention the dole office. Too depressing. She removed the chicken breasts and added some chopped onion to the pan, followed by wine and cream, finally returning the chicken to simmer slowly while she did the stir fry. Thank goodness for these handy sachets of couscous, she thought, wondering if they'd lost any nutrition in the processing. Soon she was calling everyone to the table. She had always considered it important for them to eat at least one meal a day together, to discuss the day, their plans and anything else they wanted to air.

★   ★   ★

A brown envelope arrived the next day, the letter inside informing her that an 'officer' would be calling to interview her concerning her recent claim. He or she would be calling some time the following day in the morning. How grim! She would like to be able to call and cancel the visit. She only wanted to know how much . . . if . . .

★　★　★

The following day was one of her days for the gym. Instead, forced to stay at home, she became increasingly stressed, waiting around for the 'visit'. It was half past twelve when her bell rang. Maddy opened it to find a woman with a face like a lemon standing there. Clearly written on it was a question as to why people living in such affluence should need benefits. She led her through to the kitchen.

The woman took a sheaf of papers from her briefcase, spread them on the pristine table and started to fill in a form. 'It's 'missus', isn't it?'

'What?'

'Your full name. I don't have your title.'

'Of course it's missus.'

'There's no 'of course' these days.'

By page three, Maddy's patience was wearing thin. 'I just want to know the benefit rate for someone in my circumstances.'

'We have to find out what those circumstances are. Do you have any savings?'

'I think so.'

'You should really have all the papers ready. Do your children have any savings?'

'Probably. What's that got to do with it?'

'We have to take everything into account. You'd be surprised how many people salt money away in their children's accounts and then plead poverty. It must all be taken into account.' She attempted a smile but achieved a horrible rictus.

'I'm not pleading poverty,' Maddy informed her through tight lips. 'I just want to know how I stand.'

'Do you smoke?'

'Do smokers get more?'

'No.'

'Then why ask? It's none of your business.'

Without blinking the woman asked: 'How much money do you have in your purse?'

'I haven't the faintest idea. This is clearly a bad idea. You obviously haven't a clue how much I'd get if I applied for benefits. I'd like you to leave now.'

'Just a few more questions. Do you have any, er, lodgers?'

'Only the fifteen illegal immigrants tucked away in the attic.'

'Only . . . this isn't very clever, is it? Do you want help or not?'

'Not! I told you what I wanted. Now go.'

'I'll leave you some leaflets showing how we work out your entitlement.'

'Finally! The front door's that way.'

Maddy saw the way the woman's

eyes darted this way and that on her way out. After closing the front door, she scrubbed the kitchen table and sprayed air freshener around the room.

Over lunch she looked through the leaflets and did a few sums. Heavens! That little! Nothing at all, most likely, since the lump sum from Rob 'would have to be taken into account'. No wonder some people on benefit cheated! She spent the afternoon poring over the leaflets from the university, trying to reach a decision. Not a Libran's best asset, she reflected, as she weighed up various possibilities, seeing the advantages and disadvantages — mostly the latter — in each case.

* * *

Having still not reached a decision by the following day, she set about doing some baking while Val got on with the housework. Bread dough was proving on the Aga and chocolate cakes cooling on a rack when a loud knock came on the front door.

'I'll get it,' she called to Val, who was halfway down the stairs, polishing the banisters.

'Morning, Maddy. Val.'

Liz, Rob's older sister, a successful accountant, strode past Val into the kitchen. She had Rob's lively dark eyes but she was small and lean, with a restless energy that didn't pair with her desk-bound lifestyle. 'Heard what that ridiculous brother of mine has done.'

'He called you?'

'He did not. Mm, wonderful smell! No, I called him on behalf of a client. Simon told me he'd scarpered with that flighty piece from Canada. Thought she was after Simon.'

'So did I. I'll make some coffee.' Maddy punched out a couple of loaves while the coffee filtered through and put them on the Aga to prove.

'I'll have mine in the conservatory,' said Val. 'I expect you want to talk.'

'Thanks, Val.'

'So, what are you going to do?' Liz asked.

'Well, I've considered a few options. The boys may have to go to state schools after this term.'

'Wouldn't do them any harm. Rob and I did all right in ours.'

'Jamie's not happy at the prospect.'

'He's too sensitive, that boy. Still, Hugo's been very happy at his school. Jamie'll want to follow in his footsteps. I can help. Never know what to do with my money.'

'I couldn't possibly let you.'

'Just till you get on your feet.'

'I've been going through these leaflets from the university. There's a lot of choice but I don't have the luxury of three and certainly not five years to do a degree.'

'Take a course in business management, at evening class if possible.'

'That was one of the things I was considering, but what kind of business could I run?'

'I'd have thought that obvious.'

'Not to me, it's not.'

'Start cooking professionally. Make your cakes, biscuits, quiches, flans, all the things you do so well, and sell them.'

'I wouldn't make much doing that, surely.'

'Think big. Do things on a large scale, and how about directors' lunches? Get a unit on one of those industrial estates. Val could be your first employee. You'd like that, wouldn't you, Val?'

Val, who had just walked in to collect the coffee cups, looked bewildered.

'Liz thinks I should set up a food company.'

'Good idea.'

'That's the ticket! Must dash. Glad to see you're coping. Any problems, call me, Maddy.'

'Thanks, Liz. You've cheered me no end.'

* * *

'There's a sale at school on Saturday morning,' Sophie announced as she and Dawn arrived home. 'Half to the seller, half to school funds. Why've you made so many cakes and things, Mum?'

'I was going to freeze some against hard times, or times when I'm too busy to cook. I'll take them to your sale instead. See how they go — if there are any left,' she added as the twins collected a chocolate muffin and almond Danish each.

'You can't sell food. It's for clothes and books and stuff. We're taking our old toys.'

'People have to eat, and I want to try them out for saleability.'

They rolled their eyes with a 'Mum's clearly gone loopy' exchange of looks.

★   ★   ★

The sale began at ten thirty. An hour later, Maddy's stall was bare and she had taken orders for three birthday cakes and a load of quiches for a party.

Keeping only half, she had still made a profit, and proved she could produce saleable stuff. Good old Liz.

★ ★ ★

'We can't live on the proceeds of a few cakes, though, can we, Mum?' Hugo pointed out reasonably that evening.

The others had gone to bed. Maddy smiled ruefully. 'I'd have to sell on a bigger scale, as Liz suggested, but at least I know they'd sell. We've got the money your father left and he may send more. I don't want to bank on it, though. I want to be up and running before problems loom.'

'Before he forgets us, you mean.'

'He won't do that,' she assured him, not really believing it herself.

'Out of sight, out of mind. That woman took our father. She won't stop at that.'

'Darling Hugo, don't become bitter. I'm trying not to.'

'How do you set up a frozen food company?'

'I don't know. I hadn't thought of frozen foods. What a brilliant idea! I'll find out.'

★ ★ ★

And find out she did. She rang Liz with the depressing result. ' . . . So you see, it would cost a fortune to set up. The only capital I have is the lump sum Rob left. Quite a small lump sum, in fact. That will be swallowed up by household bills in three months, I reckon, but at least the mortgage is paid off.'

'You're being very negative, Maddy.'

'I keep hitting peaks and troughs. When I think up an idea, or someone else does, I hit a peak; but when it looks impossible to achieve, I head for a trough. What shall I do, Liz?'

'Your main asset is the house. You'll have to sell it.'

Maddy felt limp with exhaustion at the mere thought. Angry, too. Selling their home from choice was one thing; being forced to do so by Liz's self-indulgent brother was quite another.

'You may be right,' she conceded, fighting back the tears.

'Go and see Simon.'

'Why? Rob has no interest in the agency anymore. Any agency would do. No point in seeing Simon.'

'There's every point. He's got the right contacts. You've got a huge asset in the house and Simon's the best agent to find you a buyer, and the right property for you to buy. You can buy something cheaper, and invest the rest in the business.'

'The kids will hate the change.'

'It's rather been forced on you. Simon will be able to find you something decent for half the price of that place.'

Visions of cramped terraces, squabbling neighbours and delinquent kids sprang to mind, mostly on pot or crack or whatever they took these days on sink estates. She knew she was being grossly unfair to the decent majority who peopled such places but she was feeling grossly negative.

* * *

On Monday, Maddy phoned Simon.

'Maddy! Great to hear from you!' Good start. 'How can I help?'

'I'm thinking, well, just vaguely considering, selling up and moving to somewhere smaller.'

'I see. Well,' he went on brightly, 'you've called the right person.'

'I'm not sure where I go from here, Simon, but Liz suggested I call you.'

'Rob's bossy sister?'

'Yes, well, I haven't had a great deal to do with her in the past but she's been very helpful since he left.'

'Probably feels guilty on his behalf. I'm really sorry about all this, Maddy. I told him he was crazy, but he seemed bedazzled by his new love. Can't see it lasting myself. Shame he needs to go to

Canada to discover that for himself.'

'Rob didn't appear to feel guilty in the slightest. He seemed to think a *coup de foudre* was perfect justification for abandoning his wife and kids.'

'It wasn't a *coup de foudre*, Maddy.'

'What do you mean?'

'Well, I took her out myself to start with, but once she'd worked out how well set up Rob was — owning more than half the agency — she began to work on him.'

'So he was a victim?' Maddy suggested wryly.

'Partly. That, and a bloody fool. What are you doing at lunchtime tomorrow?'

'Eating lunch, I imagine.'

'So if I pick you up, we could have lunch together?'

'Well, I suppose . . . '

'And discuss the kind of place you'll be looking for.'

'Thanks. I'll see you then.'

'I'll be there at a quarter to one.'

3

The following morning, Maddy arrived at Gianmarco's bright and early for her hair appointment. 'Right, Gianmarco, I want the works,' she told him. Gianmarco looked startled. He had been doing her hair for years and was used to her request for 'the usual', which meant a discreet but expert trim, barely changing in style over the years. 'Trim, streaks, blow-dry, the lot.'

'You're pushing the boat out,' he said, his accent delightfully Italian. 'Ees for special occasion?'

'I just fancy a change,' she told him evasively.

She hadn't analysed her reasons. Sure, she wanted to look presentable for her lunch date. Simon was a slick dresser and wouldn't appreciate sitting opposite a dowdy woman in faded jeans and a T-shirt, but she wasn't doing this for Simon's benefit. She didn't want to think about it too much, but probably she felt a subconscious need to show the world she hadn't become a crumbling wreck now that Rob had abandoned them. It was mainly for herself; she wasn't trying to look desperate for a man.

When she walked out of Gianmarco's, her wallet several pounds lighter, she was more than delighted with the result. The mirror told her she looked years younger. Back home she sorted through her wardrobe and pulled out a cream suit she hadn't worn for ages and a lacy camisole. As a finishing touch she added her one and only pair of killer heels. 'You'll do,' she told her elegant reflection in the cheval mirror.

At a quarter to one on the dot Simon rang the bell. When she opened the door, he did a double-take. 'Hey, you look good.' She felt good, better than in years. 'I'll tell you something — Rob must be bonkers.'

She laughed. 'Perhaps I should have

dressed up like this to do the dusting and hang out the washing.'

Of late Rob had rarely seen her in anything but jeans and T-shirts, but then how often had he taken her out and given her the opportunity to dress up? When they did go out it tended to be at a moment's notice. He would occasionally breeze in and announce he was taking her out for a meal, or whatever, leaving her no time to tart herself up. Why? she wondered now. Had he had a row with Holly, perhaps?

Today Simon had booked a table at a recently opened restaurant that over-looked the sea. Maddy had heard that it specialised in seafood. She hadn't expected to be eating there so soon.

The waiter led them to a table beside the window with a superb view of the bay. A lively sea was washing onto the long, sparsely populated beach. It was too early in the year for the bucket-and-spade brigade but there were half a dozen windsurfers following each other in circles, and kite-boarders catching every gust of wind to help them rise high into the air, defying gravity and performing seemingly impossible stunts before landing once more on the water.

'I've been wondering what this place was like. The menu looks fantastic.' She glanced at neighbouring tables. 'So does the food. What a choice. I don't know where to begin.'

'Well, how about dressed crab, followed by sea bream?'

'That sounds wonderful!'

It was, too, as was the wine, of which Maddy had more than her share.

'I have to be careful — I'm driving,' Simon insisted as he refilled her glass for the second time. Her hand lay on the table and for an instant he covered it with his. 'I've really enjoyed talking to you, Maddy.'

'Yes, but we haven't exactly talked about what we came to discuss,' Maddy reminded him, sliding her hand out of reach.

'I didn't want to spoil your appetite,' he told her, unfazed by the silent rebuff.

'What it boils down to,' she told him, steering the conversation back on course, 'is: how much will my house fetch, and how much shall I have to pay for something a bit smaller, or in a different area?'

'The first is easy. I'll have a look round and give you a valuation. As to what you buy, that depends on what sort of property you want. You mentioned starting a business. If you worked at home, you'd need some kind of work space.'

'Yes, or I could do bed and breakfast. We'd need a separate breakfast room for the guests, and more bedrooms, of course.'

'How do you think the children would feel?'

'I think the kids would prefer to stay where we are, and be just us. It's bad enough to lose their father, but to follow that by uprooting them, taking them away from their schools and friends . . . '

'How's he left you financially, if you don't mind my asking?'

'I don't mind at all, Simon. After the intrusive questions I was asked by the social security people, I'm not in the least embarrassed. As you know, Rob made a tidy sum from his share of the business. He said he'd paid off the mortgage, and put some dosh in the bank to keep us going till I get on my feet. I found out how much yesterday at the bank and I reckon it's only enough for about three months max.'

'What will you do? What did you do before?'

'I was an air hostess, for my sins.'

'Ah! Not the kind of thing you can drop back into with four teenagers.'

'I'm afraid not. Liz, Rob's sister, thinks I should go into catering but there again, to make enough to support the family, I'd need to go into it in a fairly substantial way, and it would be costly to set up.'

'Would you consider taking a unit on one of the industrial estates?'

'Actually Liz suggested that very thing. I'll look into it but it doesn't really appeal.'

'Or you could work from home if you bought a place with separate outbuildings, maybe in the country?'

A vision of rolling hills in endless sunshine sprang to mind, followed by the thought of noisy tractors and farmyard smells. Preferable to a soulless industrial unit, though.

'With that type of property — one with outbuildings — you could convert them to holiday lets, like French gîtes, or start a restaurant, or do catering for dinner parties and business lunches.'

'I feel exhausted just thinking about it. Sorry to be so negative. I did say I would consider all options, but it seems I first have to decide what those options are.'

'Or look at what you can afford and see if you feel inspired. Look, leave it with me. I'll look round your house after lunch and do a valuation. Then if you call in at the office you can see what's on the books and I'll look out for anything else that comes in — keeping all options open. Okay?'

'Thanks, Simon. Better get back to cook for the hungry hordes.'

★　★　★

'Post!' Dawn announced the following morning, plonking a heap of envelopes on the breakfast table.

'Thanks, Dawn. Help yourself to cereal and juice.' She opened a few envelopes and gave cursory consideration to their contents, mostly bills. 'Oh, Simon's valuation. He looked around yesterday after lunch.' She slit open the envelope. 'Wow! That much! Excellent! Oh, and there's a letter from your form tutor, Jamie,' said Maddy, glancing at the signature. 'Wonder what that's about. Probably a parents' eve . . . What? Jamie! She says

81

she's concerned about your absences. What absences? What's going on?'

'I don't want any breakfast — I'm going to school,' announced Jamie.

'You're going nowhere, young man, till you've explained yourself. Miss Brown wants to see me — as if I've nothing better to do. Well?'

'I don't see any point going to that school, if we've got to leave.'

'Nothing's been decided, but what did you do last Wednesday, for instance? You didn't hang around the shopping centre, did you?' Maddy had visions of unruly gangs playing truant, snatching old ladies' purses, going on a shoplifting spree.

'I came home. I don't exactly have much spending money these days, do I?'

Well that was a relief, anyway. He was still the honest little boy he'd always been, though maybe not so little.

'It won't be forever, darling.' Maddy felt guilty, as if she were the one who'd walked out, depriving her children. 'I'll ring up today and make an appointment to see Miss Brown, and we'll have a talk this evening, you and I. You're not planning to skive off today, are you?'

'He's not! I'll make sure he doesn't,' Hugo assured her. 'We'll go on our bikes.'

'We're off, too. Bye, all,' called Dawn.

'Bye!' echoed Sophie.

* * *

'So, what happened last Wednesday?' asked Hugo as he and Jamie left the house.

'It's none of your business, and I'm not going to school with you. I'm catching the bus.'

'No, you're not.'

'There's no point in going. We've only got to leave at the end of term. I don't want to change schools, and I certainly don't want to have girls in the class giggling and whispering.'

'Oh, I think I'd rather like it myself.' Hugo smiled.

'It's all right for you. Have you heard the twins' friends?' He mimicked: 'He's so good-looking, your brother. Pity you're not like him.' I hate them all!' He burst into tears, the first time he had cried in years, and Hugo realised the deep pit of misery into which his young brother had sunk.

'But you are,' he assured him, pulling his close. 'I mean, I was just like you at your age — all spots and uncertainty.'

'Were you really?'

'Of course! It goes with being nearly thirteen. How're lessons going?'

Jamie looked uncomfortable. 'I guess I'm not trying too hard.'

'Look, Mother's got enough on her plate without worrying about us. How about pulling your socks up, putting your best foot forward . . . '

'And falling flat on my face?'

They laughed at the old family joke.

'That's better. Come on, let's go.'

* * *

'To be honest,' said Miss Brown, her fringe of short iron-grey hair flopping forward as she peered over metal-framed spectacles, 'James is a disappointment. He made a good start here but now his results are barely average.'

'I find that hard to believe. He's always taken his studies seriously.'

'Well, he's not taking them seriously now. In fact, he's falling behind in maths and science.'

'Those are his best subjects.'

'So why has he stopped trying?'

'I'll talk to him.'

She didn't intend to pour out her troubles to this humourless woman. Maybe it wouldn't be such a wrench for Jamie to change schools, if he was that unhappy here.

*　　*　　*

The following day Maddy returned from Sainsbury's, laden as usual with carriers and cool bags. As she struggled to find her key without dropping anything — why hadn't she grabbed it while she was still in the car? — the door opened.

'Hi, Mum. Do you want a hand?'

She'd forgotten Jamie was at home. Legitimately today — a staff training day. He had still been in bed when she'd set off for the shops.

'Thanks, love.' Gratefully she passed him some of the bags, hoping his good mood would last. The least thing sparked him off these days.

'I'll put them down here.' He set them down on a kitchen counter, which was when she noticed his textbooks and exercise books all over the kitchen table.

'Looks as though you've been busy.'

'Yes, well, I don't want to be a dropout, whatever you think, and whatever the odious Miss Brown thinks.'

'I'm pleased to hear it. Oh, come here.' She hugged him, pleasantly surprised he didn't resist. 'Goodness,

I've just realised — you're taller than I am.'

He smiled sheepishly. 'I'm sorry I've been such a grouch.'

'You've had a lot to contend with.' She set the espresso machine going. 'Capuccino?'

'Yes please. I know it's not your fault Dad left, but I've been taking it out on you. Sorry.'

What was this — maturity rearing its ugly head? 'It's shaken us all up.'

'If we have to move, I don't mind all that much. I don't actually like that school. I don't fit in like Hugo.'

Maddy laughed. 'I certainly didn't think much of Miss Brown, to be honest. Tell you what, when you've finished what you're doing, why don't we pop in at the agency and see what Simon has to offer?'

The uncertainty of their immediate future was probably more unsettling for Jamie at his sensitive age than for the others. The sooner she made some decisions the better.

* ★ *

'Hey, this is a pleasant surprise!' Simon came round his desk and kissed Maddy's cheek, then patted Jamie on the shoulder. 'No school today, Jamie?'

'Staff training,' Maddy explained. 'We thought we'd see what you have on the books.'

'Sure. By the way, meet my new partners.' Maddy had noticed the two new faces in the outer office taking a discreet interest in her. 'This is Karen.' A forty-something with a friendly smile and mischievous green eyes shook hands with Maddy. A lacy blouse softened the otherwise severe effect of her business suit and elegant heels. Maddy felt friendly vibes from Karen — something that had never happened with Holly. 'And this is Rick.'

Rick stood up, a handsome young man in his twenties, tall and confident, with a car-salesman grin. 'Hi there. You're the former partner's — er — er . . . '

'Former wife,' Maddy volunteered with a smile.

'Sure,' he said, grinning. 'Hi!' he greeted Jamie.

'Come through to the office,' Simon suggested. 'Can I get you a coffee or anything?'

'No thanks,' she replied, and Jamie shook his head. 'We decided to set things in motion rather than let the grass grow.'

'Okay, then.' He pressed a few buttons on his desktop. 'What do you think of my new partners?'

'They seem very nice. I'm a bit surprised you've taken on two, though.'

'I had no choice. I needed the investment to pay off Rob.'

'Oh, now I feel guilty.'

'No need. He had a perfect right. The business has grown over the years we've worked together, and now he's gone I'm the senior partner, with the most say. Now then, there's this one that's just come on the market. It's comparable in size to yours but on a smaller plot, and it's in lower Parkstone. As you probably know it's a pleasant area, though not as pricey as your present address.'

'It looks lovely from the outside. What a pretty garden, isn't it, Jamie? I like the wisteria.'

'Here. Click on the screen. You can take a virtual tour through the house.'

'Oh, this is fun. What a wonderful thing technology is. Spacious hall and a fabulous kitchen. Jamie? Do you want to have a look?'

He wasn't listening, his attention caught by a picture on the wall. 'What? Oh, yes.' He came and stood behind Maddy. 'Very nice.' His gaze returned to the wall. 'Isn't that just fantabulous?'

'It certainly is,' she agreed, surprised by her younger son's sudden interest in a kitchen, however perfect. 'I like the red Aga.'

'Red? Oh, I was . . . '

She followed his gaze to the bucolic scene that had captured his attention, glanced at Jamie, then back at the wall.

'Isn't that just awesome,' he breathed. 'I'd love to live somewhere like that.'

'You would?' It was a blown-up off-sharp sepia photograph of a Georgian farmhouse surrounded by a beautiful mature garden with a backdrop of rolling meadows. 'Where is that?' she asked Simon. 'Not in Bournemouth, without a doubt. And is it for sale, or just wall candy?'

'It certainly is for sale, and it's in a little village three or four miles out of Dorchester. Would you like to see the details?'

'Well, it's not exactly . . . '

'I must warn you it needs quite a bit of work, but it's got a sound roof and it's structurally fine.' He searched through the computer files. 'Plenty of outbuildings, too, for whatever you want to do. Ah, here we are.'

In sharper focus the house clearly needed considerable TLC, but it had elegant proportions, being built of grey stone with a slate roof.

'How much?'

91

'Around half what you can expect from yours.'

'It is?'

'It is, and it's been on the market for some time, so I could probably negotiate the price down quite a bit.'

Jamie started to turn the pages, revealing high-ceilinged rooms with plaster cornices, ceiling roses, and fireplaces to die for. The sash windows had the original folding wooden shutters to exclude draughts. Outside, there was a courtyard at the back of the house surrounded, as Simon had said, by outbuildings, which looked even more neglected than the house.

'Does it have much land?' Maddy asked.

'A couple of acres.' He clicked the screen and brought up a view of gently rolling hills. 'Do you want to go and see it?'

'Oh, can we, Mum?'

'You really like it, don't you, Jamie?'

'We could have a dog.'

'Hey, not so fast. If we did, though,

you'd be the one taking it for walks.'

'Ye-es,' he said defensively. 'And we could keep a horse.'

'Steady on. Anyway, I've got to find a way of making a living.'

'But we can go and see it?'

'Of course we can.'

'Right.' Simon rubbed his hands together. 'Do you want to go now, after lunch, or when?'

'I'd love to go now, but I'd rather we all went together. Can we go on Saturday morning?'

'Very well. I'll call to arrange a time.'

They left with a rather disgruntled Jamie.

'I don't see why we can't go now. Why let the grass grow? I mean, suppose someone else buys it?'

'I have to be back for the others and, as Simon said, it's been on the market a while.' A thought occurred to her. 'Don't you usually have staff-training days at the same time as the others, Jamie?'

'I expect Hugo's revising in the

library. The sixth form's allowed to go in when the rest of us are off.'

'And the twins?'

'I don't know what their school's up to.'

'Their training days usually coincide with yours. Oh well, never mind.'

'Perhaps they're enjoying a bit of retail therapy.'

'They'd better not be, not without a word to me.'

⋆ ⋆ ⋆

'I can't believe you talked me into this,' Sophie muttered as they came to the end of another piece.

'It's fun, and look at all the coins in the hat.'

They had gathered quite a crowd in the town centre underpass. Bournemouth shoppers had never seen anything like it — two glamorous, identical blondes in low-necked gypsy blouses and colourful miniskirts, playing pop classics on violins.

'Mum'll kill us, Dawn; you know she will.'

'She won't know. And if we're going to be poor, we've got to do something.'

'How about a bit of *Hungarian Rhapsody*?' someone shouted.

'See? We're getting requests now. Smile!'

As the coins rained in, Sophie felt even more uncertain. They had reached the final bars when, with some pushing and shoving, a scruffy young man with multiple piercings and a studded jacket darted through the crowd, grabbed the hat and made off with it.

He didn't get far, fortunately. The twins were still uttering cries of dismay when a middle-aged man, smartly though somewhat ostentatiously dressed in a light suit with a garish waistcoat, stepped in front of the thief and detained him with what seemed unnecessary force.

'Yours, I believe,' he said, holding out the hat full of coins.

'How kind,' said Dawn, taking it.

As Sophie began to pack away her

violin the crowd melted away.

'You've got quite a talent,' the stranger said.

At close quarters he looked decidedly seedy, with pitted skin and a ruddy complexion. *Probably enjoyed a drink, or three*, thought Dawn, but still he *had* retrieved their money.

'Thank you.'

'Look, I'll leave you my card.' He rummaged in his pocket. 'Oh, I seem to have run out. I'm always on the look-out for talent.'

'You mean you're an agent?' Dawn asked.

'Something like that. Here's my number. Give me a ring.' He glanced round. 'Things to do.'

The next moment a young police constable came to a halt in front of them. 'What did old Dave want?' he asked.

'Well, he heard us playing,' Dawn began brightly, 'and wants to get us work, I suppose. At least, he told us he's an agent.'

'He's a pimp,' the constable informed them derisively. 'And as for you two, busking's against the law when you're blocking the walkway.'

'Oh, we're really sorry,' Sophie gabbled nervously. 'We won't do it again, will we, Dawn? We've never done it before.'

'I'd better have a word with your parents,' he said with a sigh. 'Where do you live?'

'Oh, please, don't do that!'

'Give me one good reason why not.'

'Because . . . ' Dawn began aggressively.

Sophie squeezed her arm to silence her. 'Because Mum's got rather too much to worry about without our adding to it,' Sophie said softly, her eyes filling with genuine tears.

'Tell me more.' The constable's stern expression softened.

'Dad's buggered off abroad with some Canadian slapper,' Dawn supplied starkly.

Sophie closed her eyes, inwardly

97

squirming. She opened them to find the bemused law officer doing his best not to smile.

'Listen, you two. Get yourselves off home and don't cause your poor mother any more grief. Okay?'

'Oh, thank you,' they said in unison. 'That's really cool.'

They hastily packed up their belongings, including the hat full of money, and prepared to leave. Dawn looked at the 'takings' and up at the policeman, now openly grinning.

'Look, why don't you have this for your police ball, or whatever.'

'You keep it. I reckon you're going to need it more than me.'

They could feel his eyes on their backs as they made their way out of the underpass and through the gardens.

'No more bright ideas, Dawn,' said Sophie stiffly.

'Can't promise that, but we'll keep it legal in future. Hey, he was quite dishy, wasn't he?'

'Who? PC Plod?'

'Well, I thought so.'
'Not as dishy as Mr Barton!'

★ ★ ★

'So, did you two have the day off school?' Maddy asked over supper.

'Yes, we went window shopping . . . '

'Yes, we went to the library . . . '

'What did you really do?' The twins usually either spoke in unison or Sophie left it to Dawn to act as spokeswoman.

They looked at each other and sighed. 'We went busking,' Dawn admitted.

'You what?' This was uttered with horror by Maddy, anger by Hugo and total awe by Jamie.

'How much did you make?' Jamie asked.

'What on earth did you think you were doing?' Hugo demanded.

'And where did this little display take place?' asked Maddy.

'In the underpass in the gardens,' Sophie replied quietly, tears not far away.

Maddy clapped her hand to her mouth but the next moment she was shaking with laughter. 'You two are just incorrigible,' she declared at last. 'You can't just . . . '

'That's what the policeman told us,' Dawn volunteered.

'My God! Don't say the law was involved. What did he say?'

'He sort of read us the riot act and told us not to do it again.'

'I want your word on that.'

'You have it,' came the joint reply.

Perhaps now was a good time to up sticks and move to a more gentle environment. 'Jamie and I went into the agency today. We looked at the details of a couple of properties and we're going to have a look at one of them on Saturday.'

'Great,' said Hugo. 'Where is it?'

'Well, that's the thing. It's not in Bournemouth.'

'Where, then?'

'It's not far from Dorchester.'

'But that's miles away!' cried Dawn.

'We're only going to look at it. We might all hate it. There was another one in lower Parkstone.'

'With a red Aga,' Jamie added gloomily.

'Cool.'

'And a postage-stamp garden.'

'Look, it's early days. We're just going to have a look. Okay?'

And she was anticipating having a fight on her hands. It was too much to expect that all four of them would fall in love with the place. She had her doubts herself.

All the same, she could barely repress the bubble of excitement that threatened to explode inside her.

4

On Thursday Maddy began to think seriously about moving to the country, wondering if it might create more problems. Would the children like living in a small country town, and would her own work prospects be scarcer?

With all this in mind, Maddy decided to take a trip to Dorchester to look at the town with the eyes of a resident. They had visited the place several times in the past to see the museum and look at historic sights in the vicinity such as Maiden Newton or Thomas Hardy's birthplace, but how would it be for residents actually living there?

The car was having a service, so not wanting to waste any time she went by train, arriving at lunchtime. Maybe it was the country air, but she was starving, so she began her exploration by taking lunch at the Horse with the

Red Umbrella, a bakery-cum-café named after the last production when the place had been a theatre. Her soup and roll were so delicious she decided to buy some goodies on offer to take home for the family.

The shops were a pleasant surprise. There were supermarkets, true, but there were also lots of individual clothes shops, some displaying designer clothes, others offering colourful artisan gear, which would appeal to the twins. There were also food shops offering rare varieties of tea and coffee among other things.

What a shame she'd missed the market which had taken place the day before. That was a treat to look forward to. She loved what she had seen of the town and hoped the children would feel the same — if they liked the house, of course.

After spending longer than intended trawling round the shops, she felt in need of sustenance. She found an old-fashioned tea shop in a charming little courtyard — just the place for a pot of tea and an indulgent cream cake.

To her dismay the weather had changed while she had been enjoying her refreshments, and as she left the tea shop a fine drizzle was rapidly turning to cold, persistent rain. She hurried into a nearby store and purchased an umbrella, a rose-pink one that would cast a warm glow to offset the gloomy weather. Standing in the shop doorway, she consulted her train timetable and glanced at her watch.

'Oh, hell,' she muttered under her breath.

The next train to Bournemouth left in just fourteen minutes; it was getting dark, she was cold and hungry, and she just wanted to get home.

A narrow street opened opposite. It ran in the general direction of the train station so she crossed the road and set off along it, hoping the next train, if she caught it, would be a fast one, not one of those that stopped at every tiny holt. Pity the car was in dock. Pity she'd been too impatient to wait another day so that she could drive to Dorchester.

Her mobile phone rang.

'Mum?'

'Hugo! Are you all right?'

'We're fine. A bit concerned about you, though. We found your note. When did you decide to go to Dorchester?'

'Halfway through the morning. It seemed like a good idea to look the place over, in case we decide to move in that direction.'

'When will you be home?'

'Within the hour, depending on the train.'

'Of course, you didn't have the car. Are you at the station now?'

'I'm making my way there. I can't wait to be home. The weather's turned foul but I've found a little street that I'm hoping is a short cut to the station.'

'Oh, Mum. I don't like the sound of that. Are you sure it's safe?'

'Of course, darling. This is our county town.'

'Well, take care.'

'See you.'

'Love you.'

The narrow street turned sharply round a corner and became more of an alley, made shadowy by high walls either side and so narrow here that there was just room for the width of her umbrella. Before her eyes became accustomed to the murky light and with her umbrella at a protective angle, she bumped into an object partially blocking the path.

People dumped their rubbish anywhere, was her immediate thought, but then the object groaned and stirred. It was alive and definitely human, slumped on the ground for some reason. Was it a down-and-out overdosed on drugs? She hoped not. She reached out tentatively and touched a broad shoulder, taking in the softness of quality leather, and breathing in expensive aftershave. Definitely not a down-and-out. As his head moved, a firm chin scraped her hand, a lock of dark hair fell onto her wrist and something sticky coated her fingers.

'A-are you all right?' she asked tentatively.

Daft question! Of course he wasn't. The sticky substance she was pretty sure was blood.

'What do you think?' came the irritable response.

'Sorry. Can you stand up? On second thought — ' He reached for her mobile phone. ' — don't move. I'm calling an ambulance.'

She was soon connected.

'Where are you calling from?'

'Sorry, I haven't a clue. Erm — I'm in a little road in Dorchester, actually more of an alley.' God, how feeble that sounded.

'Give me the phone,' the man muttered.

Nice voice, she thought irrelevantly as she handed him the phone for him to explain their whereabouts.

The paramedics soon arrived and took charge, to Maddy's relief. 'I'm Loraine and this is Pete. Can you tell

107

me your name?' A mutter came from the man slumped against the wall. 'What's his name, love?'

'I don't know.' Two pairs of eyes looked at her suspiciously. 'What? I found him, collapsed, here in the alley — road, whatever. I was trying to find a short cut to the train station. I think he's been assaulted.'

'Not much doubt about that.' Loraine shone her torch on a nasty gash on the side of the stranger's head. 'We'd best get you to hospital, love. What's your name?'

'Guy. Guy Deverill.'

Her partner, Pete, laid a stretcher down and settled the injured man aboard. 'Is he going to be all right?' asked Maddy.

'He'll be fine. Come on. This way.'

'Well, I wasn't planning on . . . ' For some strange reason she was reluctant to leave the man but went on, 'I need to get home to my family.'

'The police will want to talk to you. Let's go.'

So she went. As the ambulance pulled away she heard a train whistle followed by the familiar chuff-chuff of its engine. Whatever time would she get home now?

She sat in front with the driver. Loraine had to stay in the back to monitor Guy. A brief glimpse by the interior light of the ambulance had revealed a tall man of athletic build with a handsome, patrician face marred by that ugly gash on his head.

Hugo, bless him, when apprised of the situation, was quite happy to take charge. 'I'll dish something up from the freezer — feed the hungry hordes.'

They certainly wouldn't go hungry, Hugo and his three siblings. Maddy often cooked extra and kept the freezer well stocked for emergencies like this. Like this? This was totally unexpected.

She might just as well have gone home, though, for all the help she could offer.

'What happened?' asked the duty doctor at the hospital.

'Can you tell us what happened?' echoed the police when they arrived. Guy Deverill had been wheeled off to undergo tests.

'Look, I keep telling everyone, I stumbled upon him by accident. I haven't a clue what happened. I guess he was mugged. I'm sorry but I really should get back to my family.'

'Was anything stolen?'

'I'm afraid I don't know. I didn't think to ask.'

A staff nurse bustled in. 'We're just doing an MRI scan,' she said. 'Can you hang on till we've contacted a relative? You're our only contact.'

'But I don't actually know him.'

'They're bringing him back from X-ray now.'

A doctor arrived in the wake of the trolley. 'No permanent damage,' he informed Maddy, as if he was her concern.

'Good. Well, I — er — I suppose I can go then.'

The doctor looked puzzled. 'You're not his . . . ?'

'No, I'm not.'

'Sorry, Maddy,' said Guy, addressing her civilly for the first time. 'I've been a right pain, haven't I?'

'You have,' she agreed, softening slightly towards him. 'Have they contacted a relative yet?'

'My son, Dominic, is on his way.'

Not his wife, she noted — though why should she care?

'You can wait in this side room,' said the staff nurse. 'You'll be quiet in here.'

The nurses drifted away, leaving the two of them alone. The police returned to ask the victim their questions, so Maddy took the opportunity to call Hugo again. He assured her they were managing just fine and doing their homework. When she saw the police leave she went back to Guy, hoping they hadn't given him a hard time in his supposedly fragile state. Not her concern, though, was it?

'The police asked if your attackers stole anything. Did they?'

'Just my mobile phone and the ready

cash from my wallet.'

'Not your credit cards?'

'No, I only carry one and I keep it separate from my money. I can wave goodbye to my cash but the police said they may be able to track the phone.'

'It's wonderful what they can do with technology these days. Can I get you a hot drink?'

'Hopefully there won't be time. Dominic should be on his way. Why don't you hang on and meet him? He'll want to thank you.'

'For what? I didn't do anything.'

For some reason she didn't want to rush away.

He raised an eyebrow. 'For being a good Samaritan?'

She couldn't help but smile. 'Wasn't that someone who crossed a road to help? Or was it someone who didn't cross to the other side? I just bumped into you in a narrow back street.'

'You certainly did.' He grinned. 'What brings you to Dorchester?'

'We're considering moving to the

area and I decided to explore the town and see if there are any prospects of work.'

'What kind of work?'

'Something connected with food. I'm not sure what exactly. It's just about all I know.'

'Everyone has to eat. What have you been doing until now?'

'Not a lot. I was an air hostess when I met my husband. Now he's — er — we're making a few changes.'

'I see.'

She didn't suppose he did but she didn't want to bother him with her problems. He couldn't realise she felt she had been thrown overboard with only the flimsiest of paddles.

'Kids at school?'

'Yup — all four of them.'

'Quite a lot to consider then ... Sorry, it's none of my business.'

'Dad?'

A tall, handsome young man, a younger version of his father, walked into the room. After glancing at Maddy, he closed the distance to his father and grasped him in a bear hug. Guy hugged him back.

'Hey! I'm okay. No permanent damage, according to the medics. This is Maddy, by the way — my saviour. My son, Dominic.'

'Hardly. Hello, Dominic.'

'Dom, Maddy has to get back to her family in Bournemouth. I was wondering if you could drive her there.'

'No!' Maddy protested. 'I wouldn't hear of it. A lift to the station would be a help but you need Dominic here to look after you.'

'Consider it done. I'd be delighted to run you to the station, Maddy. In fact, we'll all go on the way home. It's just a tiny detour.'

At the station Dominic insisted on his father staying in the car. A train was just arriving as they arrived at the platform. 'That's lucky,' she said.

'Will you be okay?'

'Of course. You get back to your father.' Dominic looked so worried that

Maddy gave him a hug, the sort she'd give Hugo. 'He's going to be all right. The doctors said so.'

'Sure, and thanks.'

On the train journey back, Maddy had plenty of time to reflect on the strange day she'd had. What odd impulse had persuaded her to check out Dorchester as a place to live and work? Everything happened for a reason, but whatever had prompted her to cut through that alleyway? What trick of fate had caused her to collide — well almost collide — with Guy Deverill?

Guy Deverill — a nice name for a nice-looking man. She could feel the slight rasp of his skin against her hand, the softness of that lock of hair, the firmness of his cheekbone.

He was actually quite gorgeous — memorably so — but she'd probably never see him again. Soon she was home, back in the domestic routine with no time to think about the attractions of Guy Deverill.

* * *

'How much further?' Jamie asked with a yawn. Maddy's spirits plummeted — she thought Jamie had come out of his negative mood and reverted to being his old self. They did seem to be getting further and further away from civilisation as they knew it. She had just turned off a minor road and was negotiating what was little more than a narrow lane, with high banks on either side. 'This is the back of beyond.'

'I thought you were the one who wanted to see this house?' Hugo reminded him.

Remembering the letter in her bag, she realised this was probably the best chance of a fresh start they could afford. The words were seared into her brain:

Dear Mads,

I was over-optimistic in thinking I could continue to help you out financially.

Help them out!

Now we've moved to Canada . . . '
That was quick, and sooner than
Maddy had anticipated. He hadn't even
said good-bye to the children. ' . . . *As
Holly rightly pointed out, we have no
income at the moment and we shall
need every bit of capital to start an
agency or something here. We have to
live ourselves and, with a baby on the
way, Holly won't be able to work for a
while.'* So, Rob was to become a dad
once more. Maddy didn't feel shocked
or even upset. Her own children were
her only concern right now. *'At least
you have the house. It's worth a lot
now. Holly thinks you should sell it, in
which case we would expect to share
the proceeds.*

Would they indeed!

*Hope all is well. Love to the kids.
Rob*

So the old solicitor had been right.
Out of sight, out of mind. The new
'lady' in his life was leaning on him, just
as old Archie had said she would.

As Simon guessed, Holly had set her cap at the partner with the bigger income and had no intention of letting the small matter of a wife and four children come between her and Rob's bank balance. How would Rob cope with a new family? The one he'd had with her got on his nerves, and at forty-nine he had left it rather late for another foray into fatherhood. Had he any inkling of what he was letting himself in for? Starting a business in a different country with different rules and regulations: was it even possible? She almost felt sorry for him — but God, how she hated Holly.

'I think that was our turning,' said Hugo.

'Oh damn, was it?' She squinted in the rear-view mirror. 'I'll have to turn round.'

The road was only wide enough for one vehicle, with passing points along the way.

'It was just back there. Maybe there's another passing point ahead . . . '

'That would be helpful. Oh God, just look at that.'

In front of them a large tractor was trundling towards them, leaving no option but to reverse — not her best manoeuvre — or do a multi-point turn. Suddenly country living was losing its attraction. The girls started to giggle. Maddy followed their gaze — the blond, bronzed Adonis driving the tractor had escaped her attention until now. He was grinning broadly.

'Right, then,' she declared, with more decisiveness than she felt. 'Reversing it is.'

She put the Previa in reverse and backed, inch by inch, up the lane, praying that nothing was approaching from behind. It seemed an age till they reached their turning. The tractor rumbled inexorably towards them, pausing while she turned into the side road; and then moved off again, the driver grinning and giving a slow hand-clap.

'Cheeky sod,' she muttered, though

119

she couldn't help but smile as she drove off.

'Hey, this is cool,' said Hugo. The road ran uphill to a bend, then slowly downhill. Gaps in the hedge revealed stunning views of woods and fields, splashed with light and shade under the scudding clouds. 'Just look at that view.'

'Thanks, love,' whispered Maddy, adding more loudly, 'Nearly there.'

In the mirror she could see Jamie studying the scene, the scowl fading.

The road straightened, and on the left hedges and grass verges gave way to a high wall of mellow, lichen-encrusted brick. Its continuity was broken by a five-bar gate. Inside, a gravel path led to a circular drive, and beyond that stood a solid stone house with a porticoed entrance.

'We're here, guys,' she announced.

'Oh, cool!' exclaimed the twins in unison, and Maddy felt a tremor of delight and relief. 'It's vast.'

It was indeed a vast stone pile, the front porch supported by graceful columns, three shallow steps leading to a heavy oak door. Wisteria clung to the façade, and had until recently been trimmed by an expert by the looks of it.

Their wheels crunched over gravel and came to a halt at the foot of the steps.

'Who lives here?' asked Sophie, climbing out.

'No one. It's been empty for months, so I warn you, it's probably a bit musty.' She produced a set of keys and opened the door.

'Why has it been empty for so long?' asked Hugo, cutting to the chase. 'Has it got structural problems?' He looked round the entrance hall with its Poole pottery-tiled floor. Four panelled doors led off. Maddy opened the first to reveal a large reception room.

'It needs some work,' she replied, 'but isn't this a lovely room?'

It had wonderful proportions — high ceiling, long sash windows on two sides, and an original Victorian fireplace with floral tiles either side of a huge grate.

The walls were painted a traditional Georgian green with white plasterwork. The windows looked out onto a lush, overgrown lawn, tangled flower beds and boundary hedges in need of a trim.

'Not bad, is it?' Dawn whispered to Sophie.

'Just look at those cornices and the matching ceiling rose,' Maddy enthused. 'I think wall lights would be nice in here, when we get the place rewired, and can't you just picture a log fire in that hearth on winter evenings?'

'I think Mummy likes it,' giggled Sophie. 'Shall we see the rest?'

They traipsed around the ground floor together. 'This will be the dining room,' Maddy said of the large room on the opposite side of the hall. 'And this would make a cosy sitting room,' she said of a modest-sized room at the back of the house. 'This has to be the breakfast room,' she said of the fourth. 'It leads conveniently off the kitchen here.' She pulled a face. 'It has potential; that's about all you can say.

The units have certainly seen better days. Look, there's a utility room and a study . . . '

'Why a study?' asked Jamie with his customary truculence.

'Just seems like a good use for it, but any suggestions would be welcome. After all, if we're to buy it, I'd want you all to be happy here, and make your mark on the place. What do you think, Jamie?'

'I think it would make a good music room. I want to learn the cello.' The boy was a fund of surprises.

'Right, right,' Maddy agreed, inwardly groaning, knowing that cellos cost the earth; but without school fees to pay, it may just be possible. At least this room was far enough from the main sitting room for those first tortured practice sessions. 'Shall we look outside?'

Various store-rooms led off the back hall, including a wood-store and a room with shelves housing abandoned cricket bats, tennis and badminton rackets, a rolled-up tennis net and even a croquet set.

'Why would anyone leave all this stuff?' Hugo asked.

'Apparently the last occupants emigrated to Australia,' Maddy explained. 'Maybe they'd grown out of everything, or wanted to buy new.'

The back porch led out to a central path which ran between neglected lawns to a rustic arch entwined with neglected roses. They would need pruning and feeding if they were to flower this year. On a lower level were the remains of what had been a vegetable patch with vestiges of artichokes and asparagus, and assorted brassicas and roots.

'We might be able to rescue some of these,' Maddy said thoughtfully. 'Goodness, you could feed an army on a plot this size.'

'What do you know about gardening?' asked Jamie.

'I've grown enough flowers in my time, and I don't suppose vegetables are so very different to grow. They just need the right soil, the right plant food, light and warmth — but hey, what I don't know, I'm prepared to learn.'

A dozen jackdaws were viewing proceedings from the ridge tiles of a barn, making loud 'kyop, kyop' squawks.

'What a noisy bunch!' said Maddy.

'They look like little old men,' laughed Hugo. 'Look at the way they're paired up, as if they're chatting to each other.'

'That long barn could be turned into two gîtes, which would bring in some income.'

'Or your professional kitchen.'

'If you say so,' said Sophie, opening the gate from the vegetable plot to the paddock beyond. 'Ugh! Watch where you're treading. It looks as though someone's been keeping a horse here. Quite recently, too.'

'Can we have a horse?' asked Jamie.

'I'm not sure we could look after a horse.'

'You did say we could maybe have a dog.'

'It's a possibility.' And it might cheer up her rebellious teenage son. 'What kind should we have?'

'Not a silly, yappy one.'

'No, Jamie, a country type of dog.'

'How about one of those toilet-roll puppies?' suggested Hugo.

'Oh yes!' the twins enthused.

'A Labrador, yes,' Maddy agreed, happy to see the smile back on Jamie's face. 'Black or yellow? Which would you prefer, Jamie?'

'Definitely yellow,' he said at once, still smiling. 'Oh, do you think we'll get this house?'

'I think we may. We can afford it. It's around half what we can expect from our house in Bournemouth, but we'd need to get a structural survey to find out how much work needs to be done. Quite a bit, I expect. You like it, then?'

'Yes,' Jamie admitted. 'I do. The only thing is . . . '

'What, Jamie?'

'Nothing.' The sulkiness was back.

'Come on, what is it?'

'Well, Dad won't know where we are, will he?'

'You can write and tell him.'

'Have you got his address, then?'

'Not yet.' Rob had managed to write without giving one. 'He's bound to let us know soon, though.'

'Oh, bound to,' agreed Dawn sarcastically. 'At the moment *we're* the ones who don't know where *he* is.'

Hugo was the only one to notice the way Maddy's mouth tightened; the only one to understand something of the precariousness of their finances without input from Rob. He squeezed her arm. He didn't yet know about the letter. 'We'll cope. You'll soon have some business or other up and running.'

She smiled at him. She was constantly in Hugo's debt for his understanding and support. 'Of course.'

The sound of horses' hooves galloping up the field beyond the gate had them all turning towards the sound. The first horseman appeared head first, a handsome head in a

127

riding helmet, followed by broad, tweed-jacketed shoulders, an upright torso and long, lean thighs gripping a magnificent glossy black stallion. Behind him on a bay came a younger man of similar appearance, probably around twenty. They halted side-by-side a few metres away. With a jolt Maddy recognised Guy and Dominic Deverill. Guy appeared to be in excellent health, having obviously recovered from his injury, she was pleased to note.

'Maddy?'

'Guy Deverill!'

'What are you doing here?'

'I might ask you the same thing,' she replied, but with a grin. 'We're considering buying this property, and according to the details this paddock is included in the sale.'

He stared at her for a full minute. She suddenly felt unnerved. His darkly scrutinising gaze, which she met stare for stare, came from hazel eyes with interesting dark flecks. Then the lean face broke into a smile, like sunshine after a storm. He threw back his head and laughed, a rich belly laugh. 'Shall we start again?' he asked.

'Why don't we?'

He dismounted elegantly. His companion followed suit.

'Nice to see you again, Maddy.' Her hand was enclosed in a firm, dry grasp. 'I'm your, er, potential neighbour from three fields away at Deverill Manor. You've met my son, Dominic, of course.'

Her hand when released felt cold, but as introductions were made all round, she decided she must have imagined it.

'And is there a Mr Leighton?' Guy asked casually.

'Yes, but . . . '

'He's . . . ' began Dawn.

Before she could repeat the unvarnished explanation she had given the young policeman in Bournemouth, Sophie cut in: 'He's gone to live in Canada.'

Guy raised a quizzical eyebrow.

'With a woman he worked with,' Dawn added determinedly.

'Join the club,' Maddy thought she heard under his breath, but she wasn't sure.

'And is there a Mrs Deverill?' she asked anyway.

'She buggered off to Vegas to sing in some slimeball's nightclub,' Dominic declared.

'Oh God, I'm sorry. I shouldn't have asked.' The poor boy. How could any mother leave such a lovely, if outspoken, young man?

'It's fine, really. Vanessa wasn't Dominic's mother,' Guy hastened to assure her, 'and bore no similarity whatsoever to my first wife, Isabel — who died, sadly, when he was five.'

'I'm sorry.'

'Do please stop apologising,' said Guy, rather sharply. 'We were well rid, believe me, of my last wife.'

'I'm s . . . '

'So what do you think of the house?'

'Well, we haven't viewed many

130

properties, but we like the look of this one from what we've seen. Although, if we moved here, it would mean an enormous disruption in schools and friendships.'

'Of course, you live in . . . '

'Bournemouth,' she supplied.

'Quite a lifestyle change, then. Have you ever lived in the country?'

'I was brought up in rural Sussex.'

'Okay. So, what will you do with the house? I had visions of some developer moving in, flattening the site and putting up some hideous block of flats.'

'We want a home, though obviously I'll need an income, too.'

'Doing what? What do you do now?'

'Look after this lot, actually. Obviously I'll need to do more.' She didn't want to discuss her ideas with a stranger and risk the chance of him shooting them down.

'Right, well, I wish you luck. Actually . . . ' He seemed about to say more but then changed his mind. 'Come on, Dominic. We must go.'

They watched father and son remount and canter off down the field, the latter turning to salute, his eyes on the twins, before returning to the house.

'Shall we take a look upstairs?' said Maddy.

'Guess that's what we're here for,' said Dawn.

'I like the staircase,' said Sophie.

'It's beautiful, isn't it?' said Hugo, running his hand up the polished banister. 'Lovely curly end bit instead of a newel post, and very wide stairs.'

Having two turns in the staircase also allowed the stairs to be comfortably shallow. Upstairs, a long corridor ran the width of the house, with rooms leading off front and back.

'Only one bathroom,' Dawn commented. And with an old-fashioned, rusting bath and ancient plumbing.

'Yes, that's one thing we'd have to address,' said Maddy. 'We'd need at least three more, with eight bedrooms.'

'There are only five of us,' Dawn pointed out.

'True, but I've been thinking about taking in students, or doing bed and breakfast. In which case, a couple of en-suites would be a good idea.'

'Could Sophie and I have the two rooms at that end?' asked Dawn. 'We could share a bathroom and we could hide away from your students or whoever.'

'I don't see why not.' Maddy was delighted the girls were picturing themselves living here. 'We could do something with the second floor, too. It's got a solid wood floor and power points.'

'Cool,' said Jamie. 'I fancy living up there.'

They went on exploring, and falling more and more in love with the house.

* * *

For some reason the road back seemed shorter. Maddy drove in silence, listening to her children discussing the house they'd seen. 'So far, the neighbours

133

seem friendly,' she ventured.

'Mm, wasn't he gorgeous!' said Dawn.

'A bit old for you, love,' she replied. 'But yes, he was very nice.'

'I was talking about Dominic! Oh Mum, you fancy Guy Deverill!'

'Don't be ridiculous! I just said he was very nice.'

Which he was, if a bit uptight. His experiences with women would have affected his attitude and made him wary — his first wife dying, his second leaving to sing in a nightclub.

The viewing had gone far better than Maddy had hoped. She vowed to return for a more detailed look, and take an architect.

5

Once they were home, Maddy muttered an excuse and went off to her room to study Rob's letter in private. Although he'd left them, he still seemed to influence her decisions, directly or indirectly. Maddy was a fair and reasonable person by nature and Rob was relying on that. She had accepted it as fair and reasonable that he leave her the house and a sum of money to tide them over, with the promise of future voluntary payments. He had the money from the agency to establish himself in Canada — a considerable sum, according to Simon.

In the early days she had complied with his wishes, giving up work to be a housewife and thereby forfeiting her own career-building years. With hindsight she realised it had been a bad idea. The unfortunate truth was that the mortgage was not paid off — he'd lied about that, as a letter from the building society revealed, and the lump sum would only keep them going for two to three months. There was no guarantee of future payments, either. In fact, it was highly improbable. She needed to get her skates on and put her finances in order.

Simon phoned that evening. 'What's the verdict?' he asked. 'A bit rough, I imagine, compared with what you're used to?'

'We loved it.'

'You . . . no kidding?'

'No kidding. We all loved it. What I want you to do now is pull out all the stops to sell this place.'

'That keen?'

'To be honest, Simon, I have no option but to sell up. Rob hasn't been entirely honest.'

'What a surprise.'

'You don't *sound* surprised.'

'Rob has been a master of deception. Unlike me, a self-confessed lech, he had

136

us all fooled. I was a bit peeved when Holly chucked me for him but, believe me, they deserve each other. So, how're you coping, Maddy?'

'Well, it seems that the mortgage has not been paid off. I'll have to pay that from the sale of the house. The lump sum, which sounded so generous, will barely cover that and keep us going for two to three months.'

'Right, so I'll need to find a buyer p.d.q., and we'll have to negotiate the price of the one you want to buy downwards and the one you're selling upwards.'

'That's about it, Simon. I need to start earning as soon as possible, too. Apparently Holly has suggested to Rob that they should get a share of the proceeds from selling the house. I'm damned if that's going to happen.'

'Maddy, Rob got a very large sum for his share of the agency. I think you should see a solicitor and get these things tied up. Don't part with a penny.'

'I don't intend to. I've got a solicitor

who's agreed to deal with that side of things. I'll have to update him. I suddenly feel very insecure. I know I'm better off than many abandoned wives but things could so easily go pear-shaped.'

'I'll get on with advertising your house right away and, as I promised, I'll negotiate with the vendors and drive them down as low as possible. It's been on the market for ages, so hopefully they'll be amenable to lowering the price.'

'That would be fantastic, Simon.'

★   ★   ★

Several frantic weeks followed and she began to despair of ever finding a buyer. It was mid-August by the time they did. During that time, although they'd all been keen to move to the farmhouse, there were a few glitches along the way. Maddy began to question whether she was doing the right thing, forcing this enormous change on them all.

She was also concerned about whether the money would run out before the sale of their house went through. To attract a buyer, from endless television programmes she knew all about the need to dress a house and keep it clutter-free. Fortunately it was already decorated, apart from the children's rooms, in discreet, neutral tones. She dealt with family clutter day by day.

The first couple to view their home, the Johnsons, had loved it and immediately put in an offer. Maddy couldn't believe it. It seemed too good to be true — and it was. The couple couldn't get a big enough mortgage and had to drop out.

The next couple, Callum and Gail O'Shea, had argued about everything and picked fault with everything. Simon, accompanying them, maintained a tactful silence.

'Of course, we'll have to rip out the kitchen,' said Gail. 'That range is so old-fashioned.'

'It was fitted five years ago,' Maddy assured them, looking fondly at the cherry wood cabinets and gleaming range. 'I've cooked hundreds of meals on that for family and friends, and it's never let me down.'

'Yes, it does look rather tired.'

Maddy let that go, afraid she would lose her rag completely. She desperately didn't want this couple to have their home, she realised. They traipsed around the rest of it, to a litany of similar criticisms, and then went out to survey the garden. Surely they couldn't find fault here, she thought, gaining pleasure herself from the well-kept lawns and colourful, weed-free flower-beds. An enormous patio near the house was furnished with stained wood furniture and boasted a top-of-the-range barbecue and a pair of chimeneas for cooler days. There was room at one end of the terrace for their table-tennis table and a netball practice pole. Steps led down to a lawned area and further on to a section with ornamental and fruit-bearing trees.

'Oh, very twee,' Gail commented.

'It's a good-sized plot,' said Callum thoughtfully. 'How far does it extend?'

Maddy told him, alarm bells ringing at the word 'plot'. She began to suspect they were developers, for they were clearly not interested in the house as a home.

'Right then, we'll let you know,' he said.

Stung by his dismissive tone, Maddy looked at her watch. 'Goodness, is that the time?' she said. 'My next viewing is in half an hour.'

'Come on, Gail,' Callum said abruptly. 'We've got things to do.'

'Simon!' Maddy turned on him angrily as soon as she had closed the door on them. 'They weren't the slightest bit interested in the house. Or the garden, except as a plot. A building plot, I suspect.'

'I think you're right, Maddy. You don't want them to have it, do you?'

'No, I don't!'

'I'm not sure you can afford to be choosey.'

'Aren't there any genuine buyers out there?'

'Of course there are. Didn't you say you had another viewing in half an hour? And how come I didn't know about it?'

'Because it doesn't exist. I just wanted the O'Sheas out of here.'

He laughed. 'I might have guessed. Oh, excuse me, that's my phone.'

Maddy listened to one side of the conversation, which didn't make much sense. Simon switched off and turned to her, beaming.

'Well?'

'That was the O'Sheas. They're offering the full asking price. What do you want to do?'

'Isn't there anyone else interested?'

'A few, but you have to remember, it's business. If you put your property on the market and someone comes along with the money, you can hardly refuse.'

142

'But they were so critical!'

'I think initially they thought a bit of criticism would bring down the price, but when you mentioned another viewing . . . '

'What if they want to demolish it?'

'It's not your concern, once you've walked away. I suggest we let them stew for a while. As you heard, I told them the next people have put in an offer, sight unseen.'

'But that's not true.'

'But they may well have done — if they'd existed. It happens, so it's only a small lie.'

Maddy laughed. She hadn't taken to those two at all. 'Okay.'

The next genuine viewers were interested, and the next. In the end a couple Maddy had really taken to surprised her by trying to better the O'Sheas' offer. They were Jon Mathers, an airline pilot who worked out of Bournemouth International Airport, his wife Alice, a former air hostess, and their three delightful children.

'I just love it,' Alice had said. 'I could see us living here very happily.'

'So could I,' Jon agreed. 'It's by far the nicest house we've seen, and we'd like to go for it.'

'There's another party offering the full asking price,' Simon told them.

'Oh. Does that mean we have to better it?' Jon Mathers had asked.

They looked so disappointed that Maddy stepped in. 'No, I'd like you to have it. You do want to live in it as a family home?'

'Well, that's the idea. What else?'

'I think the other people wanted to knock it down and put up a block of flats.'

'Oh, that would be sacrilege. It's such a comfortable house; it's got a real family feel. What's more, we could move in just as it is. We can decide, once we've lived here for a while, whether to make any changes.'

And so it was agreed. The Matherses came round occasionally after that, always phoning first, to check on something or measure up for furniture.

'How long before we can move?' Maddy asked Simon a couple of weeks later.

'Have patience, Maddy. These things take time, as you should be well aware.'

'I don't want time to get cold feet, or for the children to decide we've done the wrong thing.'

'I'm sure it will go through before the autumn term. After all, there's no forward chain your end, is there?'

'That's true.'

Liz turned up unexpectedly one morning, and Maddy gave her a brief résumé of their plans. 'Well, that is good news,' she said. 'Has that brother of mine been in touch?'

'Not since his letter telling me not to expect any more money from him.'

'I'm sorry, Maddy. Is there any way I can help?'

'We're fine, thanks, Liz. Just waiting for completion, so that we can move in and get cracking on the new place.'

'Pity you can't make a start while it's

still empty. It's difficult to do wiring and plumbing once you're living there.'

'That's true. Maybe I should contact the other side.'

*   *   *

A few days later Maddy was in the middle of a baking session when the doorbell rang. Wiping her floury hands on her apron and pushing her hair back, she hurried to the door, wondering who it could be. She certainly didn't expect the man who stood there, looking slightly sheepish.

'Guy!'

'I would have phoned,' he explained, 'but I didn't have your number.'

'You had my address, though, apparently.'

'I contacted the agency.'

'But . . . '

'We need to talk. May I come in?'

She stood back, allowing him to enter, and led the way to the kitchen where she hastily retrieved a tray of bread rolls from the oven.

'Mm, delicious smells. You are busy.' He reached up and brushed a finger slowly down her cheek. A delicious sensation uncoiled deep within her and her eyes flashed in alarm.

'Smudge of flour,' he told her with a grin.

Annoyed with herself for her reaction, which she hoped he hadn't noticed, she asked sharply, 'What did you want to talk about?'

'It's about the house you want to buy.'

'Is there a problem? We're not the neighbours you'd prefer?'

'Nothing like that. I should have declared an interest sooner.'

'Declared an interest? That sounds a bit legal or official or something.'

'The thing is, Maddy, I own the house.'

'What? But why didn't you . . . '

'I was so astonished to see you and your family there as potential buyers, I couldn't bring myself to say anything. I realised that was unfair and it started me thinking about what I really want.'

'Coffee?' She held a pot of newly brewed coffee over two mugs.

'Please.'

'Help yourself to a biscuit — stem ginger.'

'Mm, delicious. Tell me why you want to move to the country and why that particular house?'

'Why not? We love the location. It needs a bit of work but we can manage that.'

'You've clearly made this house the perfect family home. Why leave it?'

'Okay. To be frank, we can't afford to stay. It's worth a lot — twice the price of your house in its present condition. We could buy that and spend a sum on renovations.'

'Or you could rent it from me until you're sure it's what you want. It has always been rented till now. It's part of the estate, part of Dominic's inheritance; but as he's an only child, he'll be happy to make our present home his one day. It wouldn't be a high rent and I would take on any renovations you think necessary.'

'I didn't realise that was an option.' It sounded like a wonderful offer but Maddy could see drawbacks. 'We'd want to make the house our home, and once the children have moved schools we wouldn't want to up sticks for a good few years. Anyway, what did you mean about what you really want?'

'I meant I'm not entirely sure I want to sell. That house has been part of the estate for a very long time and Dominic may want the option of living there one day.'

'I see. Well, I don't really. I'm looking for a home which gives us some security for the children. A rented house seems a bit scary.'

'But you and your family could move in now and you could take a long lease on it. Your capital would be intact if the time came for you to move on.'

'You sound as though you'd like us to move in.'

His expression became guarded. 'It doesn't do a house any good staying empty. It's a while now since the previous tenants left, so you'd be doing me a favour living there.'

'Well, that's a lot to take in — a complete change of direction, really. I'll think about it and discuss it with my solicitor. It would certainly give me breathing space and the funds to set up a business of some sort.'

'I didn't mean to create more problems for you, Maddy.' She liked the soft way he said her name. 'Think about it and I'll be in touch soon. Here's my card with phone numbers and stuff.'

They stood up at the same time. Their eyes met briefly and she looked away, afraid of what she might reveal in hers. They crossed the hall to the front door. Maddy opened it and waited for him to leave. He paused, then swivelled to face her. Leaning down he kissed her cheek, his lips warm and firm against her skin.

'I'm sure we'll work something out to suit us both,' he murmured, his wonderful flecked brown eyes inches from hers.

'I'm sure we shall,' she agreed quietly, averting her eyes from the fire in his and wishing he'd step back before she exploded from the fire ignited by his nearness.

The next moment he tilted her chin and kissed her lips for a millionth of a second. 'Sorry, Maddy, I couldn't resist,' he said — and then he was gone.

She touched her fingers to her lips. That briefest of kisses had been all she had imagined and more. Now something had changed between them and the mere thought of him set her pulses racing. Was it a good start for a landlord/tenant relationship, though?

'Mum! What are we having for dinner tonight?'

Jamie was home; reality was restored.

★ ★ ★

151

True to his word, after mutual discussion, Guy had the house rewired and lots of additional sockets installed. He also engaged a firm of plumbers to do a first fitting ready for the new bathrooms and en-suites they had decided on.

Simon helped by recommending a removal firm used to dealing with large households. On the appointed day, two enormous vans turned up and Maddy, apart from instructing the team on which items were to go into storage or to a saleroom, was relegated to the task of serving tea, coffee and refreshments while the five men and one woman got on with the job of packing their treasured belongings. With only the essential pieces going straight to the house, the plumbers and decorators would be able to get on with their work.

And so they moved in.

'Can we choose our own carpets and curtains?' asked Sophie, seated on a tea chest at their new home, flicking through swatches of fabrics.

'Within reason,' Maddy agreed, anxious for them to make it their home.

So, room by room, the place took shape.

'I think I'm going to like it better than our last place,' Dawn declared to Maddy's relief.

It was Saturday and they had been there a fortnight, getting used to living with the sound of hammering and drilling as the bathrooms were completed, when a Smart car turned into their drive.

'Who on earth can that be?' Maddy wondered aloud from the landing, where she watched, as a tall, rangy man in his mid-thirties unfolded himself and stood up. He surveyed the house for a moment, flicking a college-type scarf over one shoulder.

Maddy ran downstairs to open the door, scooping up a pile of letters before she did so. 'Good morning.'

'It is indeed.' He proffered a hand and shook hers firmly before unwinding the scarf to hang either side of his neck.

'Robin Groves, your local vicar.'

Who had a deep, resonant voice, no doubt good for singing hymns, and a charming smile that lit dark-lashed green eyes in a strong, friendly face.

'Oh, good morning. Maddy Leighton.' Who hadn't been to church for ages. 'Do come in.'

He followed her across the hall and into the kitchen where Hugo and the twins were lounging around the table having elevenses and cookies, and playing a half-hearted game of Scrabble. Jamie's efforts on the cello could be heard from the newly christened music room.

'Ah, the family are all here, too. How nice.'

'Three of them. The fourth, as you can hear . . . '

' . . . is murdering our eardrums with the cello,' said Hugo with a smile.

'You have to start somewhere,' said the vicar.

'Timbuktu would be nice,' suggested Dawn.

'Coffee?'

'Thanks. So, how do you like living here so far?'

'It's early days but I love it already,' Maddy told him.

'Can we hope to see you in church?'

'We-ell, to be honest, we're not exactly regular worshippers.'

'More the hatches, matches and despatches type,' Dawn explained helpfully.

'Right, well, most of the villagers find it's a good place to meet their neighbours and we do put on social events, flower festivals, cheese and wine suppers, and so on, which I announce during the service. Maddy, why don't you come to the next parish council meeting? It's at the vicarage on the first Wednesday in September. Also as I cover three parishes, there's only one service a month at the local church. It's at three o'clock on the third Sunday of the month.'

'I'll put it in the diary.'

'Mm, excellent coffee. I understand

you're starting a catering business?'

'That's the plan.' Word certainly spread in the country. 'Try a cookie — they're homemade.'

He bit into one. 'Very nice, too. Stem ginger?'

The last time she'd made some was at their old home when Guy had called and sampled them. 'It is.'

'Delicious.' He cast an eye over the Scrabble board. 'Whose turn is it?'

'Mine,' Sophie replied.

'Let's have a look at your tiles. You don't mind?' he asked the other two, who were stunned into silence. 'You've got a winner there,' he told Sophie.

'Where?'

'Do you mind?' he asked again.

'Well, yes,' said Dawn.

'Be my guest,' said Hugo, simultaneously.

'You have space, p, space, p, space, e, space, y.'

'I don't see . . . ' began Sophie.

'Neither do I,' added Dawn, who had

decided it was fair game to take a peek. 'Oh, peppery.'

'I don't have a third 'p',' said Sophie, 'and Robin wants to use the space before the first 'p', don't you? Go on, then, but I don't suppose it'll be right.'

'Oh, I think it is,' Robin said with a smile. 'I'm just rather afraid someone may suffer it.' He proceeded to lay out Sophie's tiles to form the work 'apoplexy'.

'Oh, very good,' said Hugo.

'Yes, very good,' Dawn mimicked, 'but you can't have it, Sophie.'

'Why not?' asked Sophie.

'Because it wasn't your idea.'

'You didn't object before he said what it was.'

'Yes, I did.'

'Not really.'

'Oh dear, I fear I've opened a Pandora's box. Perhaps I'd better go.'

Dawn scowled while Hugo tried not to laugh.

'It was nice to meet you,' Maddy told him, with a smile.

'You, too. See you all in church?'

'Maybe.'

'Do any of you play chess?' Robin asked, putting his head back round the door.

'Is the Pope Catholic?' asked Dawn, putting a wry smile on Robin's face. 'Oops!'

'We all play a bit, but Jamie and I take it more seriously,' Hugo explained. 'If you ever fancy a game, give us a shout.'

'You're on.'

'It's okay!' Dawn called after him. 'Robin?' He turned. 'It was only a game,' she said with an unusually charming smile. 'And I'm not at all apoplectic.'

'Phew! I thought I'd blotted my copybook on our very first acquaintance.'

'Of course not. See you in church.'

'Oh, I almost forgot, Maddy. My parents are coming down next weekend. I came to ask if you could rustle up a meal for the Saturday evening.

Mother will want to do Sunday lunch herself.'

'I'd love to. Shall I drop in a menu?'

'I can tell you what they'll want now. They would enjoy some homemade soup, white fish of some kind with a nice sauce, young vegetables, and a choice of steamed pud or fruit salad.'

'That sounds straightforward. Cod, haddock, turbot?'

'Cod or haddock. Definitely not turbot.'

They shook hands and she returned to the kitchen. 'That was magnanimous of you,' Maddy told Dawn after seeing Robin out.

'Yes, well . . . I mean, he was kind of cute.'

'You're incorrigible,' said Hugo.

'And he's not the celibate sort of cleric, is he?'

'I guess not.'

'Another customer,' Maddy told them gleefully. 'And I've got two orders for birthday cakes and one for a golden wedding.'

'Fantastic. Are they the result of your advert in the local paper?'

'Presumably.'

*   *   *

Later that evening, she sat down and tried to make sense of their financial situation. She could charge top prices for top-quality food. With a pang she wondered if their young vicar could afford it, and decided he couldn't. She'd give him a discount.

The cooking side of things was going well but, as they were only renting, she couldn't contemplate converting the outhouses to provide gîte accommodation. A lodger might help. The kids wouldn't like one living in, was her next thought. She'd have to vet them carefully.

*   *   *

Maddy's reputation spread with each cake she delivered. With a few more dinner parties they could just about manage. She went to the parish council meeting at the vicarage, where someone mentioned a christening cake she had made, praising it to the skies and bringing in another order.

Guy was there, at his most solemn and business-like, talking about some covenant set up by one of his forebears and discussing how best to use it. He barely acknowledged Maddy's presence, which she found hurtful, though she knew she had no reason to.

Liz breezed in a few days later, parking her Porsche askew on the drive. The children were all variously practising their musical instruments, doing homework or arguing in another room.

'Well, how's everything working out, Maddy? Are the kids settling in all right at school?

'Very well, actually. I think they're enjoying all being at the same school, a mixed one of course. Jamie's still lagging behind in maths, though.'

'Get him some one-to-one. He'll soon catch up.'

'Good idea. I'll just lay the table. You will stay for a meal?'

'Try and stop me, but I'll lay the table; you get that delicious-smelling casserole out of the oven. Are we eating in the kitchen?'

''Fraid so. The dining room's not done yet. Nor, actually, is the casserole. It'll be another half-hour. Time for a glass of wine.'

'Excellent! How's the catering coming along?'

'Slowly, but it's gathering pace. What it boils down to is a few special occasion cakes and the odd dinner party in the client's home.'

'Mm.' Liz sat down at the kitchen table and whipped out a pad and pen. 'Let's work out some figures.'

Maddy groaned inwardly as she fetched a bottle of chilled white wine and took the seat opposite. As she poured the wine into two glasses, she listed the orders she'd had. Liz started talking about costs and marketing and even mentioned income tax.

'I don't think I'll be paying tax yet. It doesn't amount to much, Liz, does it?'

'You certainly won't get rich on that much work.'

'Tell me about it.'

'Well, it's obvious you can't do much professional cooking here. However, you could consider what you have done already as market research. Have you had any complaints?'

'No, I'm thankful to say.'

'Have you had any special praise for any item?'

'Everything's gone down really well. There was a problem getting the timing right at one client's house, because I wasn't used to the antiquated cooking range.'

'How did they take it?'

'Very well, I suppose. In fact, the wife was delighted to be able to demonstrate the need for a new cooker to her rich but stingy husband.'

'It's not the answer, though, is it?

You'll need to decide which lines are your best and likely to sell well. Have you looked into taking a unit, as we discussed, on one of the new industrial estates? You could still do individual parties but you could do high-quality ready meals and so on to sell to supermarkets.'

'You make it sound easy.'

'Nothing's easy in business, but you can do it. I know you can.'

Maybe she could, but did she want to run a serious business? Her main concern was providing a stable home for the children, and that meant being there for them as she had always been. How could she if she was slaving away somewhere else? Liz didn't have a clue about being a parent.

6

Maddy hummed softly to herself as she applied the last sugar rose. The golden wedding cake, her latest creation, was for the Upshalls, a couple who lived in the village. She took a pace backward to admire it.

'Yup, they're going to love it,' she told herself.

Had she spoken aloud? Well, what if she had? *Who cares?* she asked herself. She loved the blissful quiet of living in the country, with neighbours a couple of stones' throw away at the very least and the sound of traffic a distant hum.

A shadow filled the open doorway and fell across the room, cutting out the light. She swivelled round, startled. On sunny autumn days like this she left the door open to admit light and air, the sound of birdsong, the baa-ing of sheep in the middle distance, and the muted drone of the occasional tractor ploughing the rich Dorset earth.

'Sorry, I didn't mean to alarm you,' came the deep and, yes, sexy voice of Guy Deverill, his tone slightly amused, to her annoyance. So he'd heard her talking to herself. So what?

'I didn't hear your car — or your horse,' she said with some asperity.

'I tramped across the fields — it's such a fabulous morning for late September. I say, that looks good — most professional. Oh, I'm sorry.' He looked down at his booted feet. 'I'm treading mud all over your floor.'

'Don't worry. At least it's dried mud at the moment. I haven't got the kids trained yet, so I'm getting used to it. These tiles are very forgiving anyway, although it was a shame to cover the old worn flagstones.'

'I like what you've had done here.' She always ran her ideas past Guy, who was paying the bills since it was, as he said, his house and he and Dominic would therefore benefit from the changes in the long run. 'It's a beautiful kitchen. How's the rest of the house coming along?'

'Slowly, but it's going to be lovely thanks to you. Would you like some coffee?'

'I'd love some, although this isn't just a social call.'

Maddy felt a dart of something she could have construed as disappointment. *Get a grip*, she told herself, tipping coffee beans into the grinder.

'That really is a wonderful cake. Is it for anyone I know?'

'It's for the Upshalls at Higher Moreton cottages.'

'Of course, Jim and Grace. The names should have given me a clue.'

He leaned over and picked up a petal lying beside the cake, discarded. He was about to lift it to his mouth when Maddy, without thinking, lightly slapped his wrist. She gasped, appalled at herself but, before she could apologise, he had reached around her and seized her wrist, swivelling her to face him. There was laughter in his eyes as they stood inches apart. She looked up apprehensively. His thick, unruly dark hair fell over his brow and at close quarters, she could see a tiny black speck close to his right pupil, his eyes not brown but a glorious shade of amber.

He laid his hand against the side of her face and she felt the most shocking but delicious dart of wanton lustfulness. Her body surged towards his, wanting to settle her soft curves against his muscular leanness. She noted an echoing daze in his eyes and wondered afterwards what would have happened had the post-box not rustled at that moment with a large delivery of post.

She excused herself, pink with confusion, to collect it from the hall. Flicking through, she noted an envelope with her solicitor's name on. She would open that one first when she was alone. For the moment it would remain with the rest on the hall table.

Back in the kitchen, she finished

making the coffee and set out two large cups and saucers. Guy took a seat at the table and watched her every move.

'How do you like your coffee?' she asked quietly.

'Just a dash of milk.' He took a sip. 'Mm, superb.'

'You said this wasn't a social call,' she reminded him.

'I said it wasn't just a social call,' he reminded her in turn.

'Okay, so . . . '

'Nor did I intend what nearly happened just then to happen.' He paused. 'However, I'm not sorry it did — almost happen, and I may well make more frequent social calls just for the coffee.' He grinned. Her first impression of him as uptight and arrogant couldn't have been more wrong. 'No, I was wondering, if you aren't too busy, if you could do the catering for the next church do.'

'What kind of do?' She had visions of a bun fight in the local village hall.

'Those of us with sizeable houses take

it in turns to give a party in aid of church funds, inviting all the locals.'

'Robin mentioned something about cheese and wine parties.'

'You've met our local vicar?'

'Yes. He almost started world war three interfering in a scrabble game,' she told him with a laugh.

'That sounds like Robin. Anyway, to get back to the church do. Robin will announce it on Sunday and it will be in two weeks' time on the Saturday. It's ticket only and you can deduct food costs from the proceeds. The rest goes to church funds for repairs, et cetera.'

'You want me to hold it here?' she asked with dismay. 'This is one of the few finished rooms . . . '

'No, of course not. For one thing, you haven't volunteered . . . '

'I may do, in future, but, as of now . . . '

'Of course. Sorry, I didn't make myself clear. It's actually my turn and frankly my housekeeper isn't up to it. She can cope with plain family meals and that's about it. Dom and I often eat out to get a bit of variety. For the church parties I usually get in a load of Waitrose party goodies when it's my turn to play host, but it would be wonderful to have a proper caterer.'

'A proper caterer! I like the sound of that. I'm still a novice but it's what I've set out to do, so yes, I'll give it a try. I'll be inviting criticism, I suppose.'

'But you could also be drumming up custom.'

'That would be nice! Do you want me to come up with ideas, or will you give me a list, or . . . '

'Why don't you all come over for supper one evening and we can discuss it.'

'That would be lovely.'

'How about this coming Friday?'

'Yes, I think Friday's all right with everyone.'

'Good. How are the kids settling in at school?'

'They're very happy there, except perhaps Jamie. He still misses having his father around, even if Rob was conspicuous by his absence of late and took little interest in Jamie. He threatens to go after his father in Canada from time to time. He's getting poor marks at school, too, especially in maths, which used to be his best subject.'

'Sounds like he could use a bit of extra tuition.'

'That's what my sister-in-law suggested. Where do I find someone, though?'

'Start with the school.'

'Thanks. There's a parents' evening on Tuesday; I'll look into it then.'

Once Guy had left, Maddy retrieved the pile of letters and picked out her solicitor's long white envelope. With shaky fingers, she opened it and read the bold message that she was now eligible for her decree nisi, with a suggestion that she make an appointment to see her solicitor. She was surprised at the hot prick of tears in her eyes, followed by the realisation that her sadness was for what might have been, what should have been and certainly not for what had been.

★   ★   ★

It was Maddy's first parents' evening at their new school, for Jamie's year, and she was feeling distinctly nervous. She needn't have worried. The teachers she had elected to see rated her youngest son above average to excellent. Jamie's maths teacher was her last but one appointment. She parked herself on the chair outside his classroom and waited with some trepidation. What would he be like, this dry old maths teacher Jamie didn't get on with? Or so she'd gathered from Jamie's remarks. The last parents, a couple, came out smiling.

'Mrs Leighton? Jamie's mother?'

Maddy nodded. 'Mr Carter?' she asked with some astonishment.

Mr Carter was neither dry nor old, were her first impressions. On the contrary, he was a very fit young man in his mid- to late-thirties, at a guess, and a shade over six feet, with an athletic build. His smile was genuine yet there was something there, some shadow of experience behind a pair of beautiful dark blue eyes.

'Andy Carter,' he confirmed, taking her hand in a firm grip. 'Take a seat.'

'I'm Maddy,' she said as he closed the door and she sat on one of the parents' chairs.

'Is there a Mr L?'

'There is, but not with us as such.'

'Mmm.' He stroked his lean chin thoughtfully. 'Does Jamie see his father?'

'Rob left us and went off to Canada, so no, he doesn't.'

'That could explain it.'

'Explain what?'

'I get the feeling Jamie's mind is often elsewhere. If I ask him a direct question, he's spot on with the answer. He understands the concepts of maths but when it comes to the written stuff, he makes a lot of careless errors.'

'Maths used to be his best subject.'

'I can believe that, but now he needs to become more focused.'

'So it seems. Someone suggested he might benefit from one-to-one tuition. What do you think?'

'It always helps, but it can be expensive. I don't want to pry, but would that be a problem?'

'Life's full of problems. I've learnt to prioritise. I'll just have to bake a few more cakes.'

'Cakes?'

'I've started a catering business, so yes — cakes, dinner parties, et cetera.'

'Mmm,' he said again. 'How would you like to do a deal?'

'Such as?'

'I could offer my services as young Jamie's tutor in exchange for a square meal.'

Maddy burst out laughing. 'Are you serious?'

'Never more so! Is it a deal?'

'You're on! When's a good night for you?'

'How about Friday?'

'Okay. Oh, hang on, Friday, I'm seeing someone to discuss a catering job, though normally Friday would be fine.'

'Or Thursday, or Wednesday, or Tuesday . . .'

'How about Thursday this week and Friday after that?'

'That suits me.'

'What sort of food do you like?'

'I'm not fussy, or vegetarian, or anything. Anything home-cooked, not pre-packaged, would be wonderful.'

'No problem. Eat at seven, tutoring afterwards?'

'I'd rather it was the other way round — tutoring first, save the best till last.'

'You're on. I'd better go. I'm seeing Jamie's French teacher next — my last appointment.'

'Nice to have met you, Maddy. See you on Thursday.'

'Shall we say six thirty, eat at seven thirty?'

What have I done? she asked herself

as she drove home. She'd invited one of Jamie's teachers into their home. How embarrassing was that? How would Jamie react? She anticipated the worst.

★ ★ ★

Jamie reacted with the expected truculence. 'You've done what? I can't believe you'd do that! What, Mr Carter's coming here? On Thursday? Well, don't expect me to be here. And you've actually invited him to eat with us?' And on and on and on.

Thursday evening arrived. As did Andy Carter — to the giggling delight of the twins, who had transferred their crush on their French teacher at their old school to the handsome maths teacher at their present one.

Jamie wandered down from his room, unsmiling, but at least he saw fit to grace them with his presence. 'Mr Carter,' he greeted him tersely.

'You can call me Andy strictly out of school, Jamie, if it makes things easier.'

'We can use the dining room.'

'Fine. Oh, Maddy, I brought a bottle of wine. Is that all right?'

'Fantastic.'

Maddy watched the door close, all fingers crossed, and went off to chambrer the red wine and finish the meal.

At seven thirty on the dot she tapped the little brass gong they had set up in the hall. It sounded throughout the house to let everyone know a meal was ready. Hugo and Dawn came down together. Sophie was already laying places on the large oak refectory table in the kitchen. Jamie appeared a few minutes later followed by Andy Carter.

'Mm, that smells wonderful.' He sniffed appreciatively.

'Would you like to sit here?' She indicated the chair to her right. Anticipating the girls' jostling to sit beside him, she went on: 'Hugo, you sit at the end, Jamie next to Andy . . . ' Scowl, scowl from the twins. 'And girls,

178

you sit opposite. Everyone all right with that?'

It seemed so, apart from 'But I usually sit there,' from Dawn to Sophie, who had taken the chair opposite Andy. They were nothing if not subtle, her girls.

'All right, love?' Maddy asked Jamie as she put a bowl of leek and potato soup in front of him.

'Fine.'

'More than fine,' Andy added. 'He's very good at maths. Sometimes if there's a change — a change of school, there's a bit of a knowledge gap in maths due to the style of teaching, the different approach. But with talent like Jamie's, he'll soon catch up.'

'Wonderful!'

It wasn't costing money, either, and Andy seemed to appreciate the meal and the family ambience.

'So what's Mrs Carter doing while you're here?' asked Dawn.

Maddy winced, suspecting there were aspects of Andy's life he preferred to keep private; she guessed she was right, from the way he froze for a split second and turned pale.

'There isn't a Mrs Carter,' he told them quietly. 'She died in childbirth. They both did.'

'Oh God, I'm sorry,' said Dawn, appalled.

'It's all right. It's probably best to be open about it. We knew it was risky but she so wanted a baby.'

'And now you've got nothing,' Sophie whispered, her eyes filling.

'Hey, that's enough of my sadness. It's been three years and I've learned that life has to go on. Of course, it's different, and I miss her still. Serena was such a bright and bubbly girl. She used to paint — children and animals, mainly. She told me if things went wrong she wouldn't want me to grieve for ever.'

'And has that helped?' asked Maddy, handing him a plate of sliced roast pork, while the girls set vegetable dishes and sauce boats on the table.

'I've kept busy. Apart from teaching I play a lot of sport and, for my sins, I'm writing a novel.'

'How exciting!'

'I don't know about that. I've almost reached the end, but I've suffered almost constant writer's block.'

'Yes, it must be difficult to do something when it depends on self-motivation.'

'Exactly! At least, that's what I tell myself. Self-discipline is the answer, and finding a quiet corner.'

'Is that a problem?'

'Sometimes. I have a small flat on the top floor of a house in town. The family below have produced two sprogs since I moved in, and although they're delightful kids, they're not always quiet, day or night.'

'I wonder how Dad's going to cope when his floozie has hers?' Dawn smirked.

'Dawn!'

'Well, he didn't like the noise we made, Mum. 'Do they have to play the piano now?'' she mimicked. ''Can't they use the practice pedal? Does that boy have to stamp upstairs? Why do they have to slam doors?''

'Sorry,' Maddy apologised. 'It's all still a bit raw.'

'So, you'll be having a new sibling? How do you feel about that, Jamie?

'I think it's gross. Disgusting. I hate them all.'

'Understandable. Time's a great healer, though, believe me. It may be a cliché but it's true. You move on, take up new challenges, make new friends. Do you see anything of your Dad?'

'Hardly! They went off to Canada, where she came from, and he hasn't been back.'

'Nice bit of pork, Mum. Is it from that organic farmer in the next village?'

Bless you, Hugo, for changing the subject.

'Yup. I usually go there now.'

'Nothing beats locally grown produce,' said Andy. 'That's one of the joys of living in the country.'

'You're right. The applesauce is from our own Bramleys, which are just ripening, but we haven't got round to growing our own vegetables. That's something I intend to plan this winter.'

'My parents have got a market garden up in Worcestershire. If you ever need plants or a garden plan or anything, just shout.'

'I'll bear that in mind.'

* * *

'We're invited to the Deverills' tonight,' Maddy told them over breakfast the following morning.

'Oh Mum, you said we could go to Bournemouth and stay over with Stacey,' said Dawn.

'This weekend?'

'Well, we didn't exactly specify which weekend, but I've told Stacey it's okay for tonight.'

'What are you planning to do in Bournemouth?'

'There's an under-eighteen disco in town. We thought we'd go there.'

'And it's all right with Stacey's parents to stay?'

'Of course.'

The twins had often stayed overnight with friends and vice versa when they lived in Bournemouth. It had seemed easy when they were all a short taxi ride away. Now Maddy felt uneasy, as if the umbilicals were stretching a mite too far, too soon. She'd better check with Stacey's mother, Penny.

'Hi, Penny.'

'Maddy! That is you, isn't it?'

'It is.'

'How are you? Not checking on the girls' plans, are you?' Penny was laughing, knowing very well what Maddy was doing. 'Look, it's fine. We're looking forward to having them. We haven't seen the twins for ages.'

'Thanks, Penny. It's very kind of you to have them both. You must all come out for Sunday lunch one weekend. We're gradually getting straight.'

'We'd like that — a bit of decent grub!'

'I'll see how everyone's fixed and we'll do that soon. What's the latest gossip from the big city?'

It was good to have a natter but Maddy soon found herself getting bored. She was living on a more basic level these days and talk about the goings-on of the smart set in which Penny moved seemed somehow trivial by comparison. Her thoughts started wandering to those garden plans Andy had mentioned and to the pleasant prospect of eating at the manor that evening.

★　★　★

'Now, girls, are you sure Penny will meet you at the other end?' Maddy asked as she put them on the train in Dorchester.

'Yes, Mum. She promised. I don't know why the fuss,' Dawn declared. 'We could easily get a bus from the interchange, but Penny insisted.'

Good for Penny. 'And have you got enough money?'

'Plenty, really,' Sophie assured her. 'We just need our entry money for tonight.'

'And a bit for a spot of retail therapy tomorrow,' put in Dawn.

'Take this, just in case,' Maddy insisted, handing a twenty-pound note to each of them.

'Thanks, Mum. We won't waste it.'

They'd all been so good, accepting their new precarious status with little complaint. She waved them out of the station and turned to drive home, wondering what to wear that evening. How smart? How casual?

In the end she thought she had struck the right note. She wrapped a burgundy shawl round a cream wool dress, proof against the cold of an old manor house, and twirled in front of the cheval mirror in her bedroom. Hair up or down? Halfway up, she decided, pinning it with a large gold and dark red clip. Heels but not killer heels. She had aimed for and achieved under-stated elegance.

The boys appeared, showered and groomed, in their best casuals. What a credit they were to her. What a lot Rob had turned his back on. His loss.

Maddy was relieved to find Guy dressed in a similarly relaxed fashion, black sweater and cream chinos, and looking pretty yummily handsome, she thought to herself.

'It's just me,' Guy said. 'Dominic's gone to see some mates from his old school.'

They stood around in the drawing room, chatting, till Mrs Frimley tapped on the door. 'Supper's ready,' she told them.

They decamped to the dining room, a darkly panelled room with sumptu-ous, if rather ancient, drapes. It was the first time Maddy had seen the room and she looked round curiously but discreetly. She suspected the furniture, with its intricate carvings on chairs and side tables, was probably priceless, though it, too, was shabby and in need of some tender loving care. The velvet of the floor-length curtains had probably once been a rich rose colour but was now dusty and faded on the folds.

Mrs Frimley wheeled in the trolley and set a vast lidded tureen in the centre of the table. Vegetable dishes, similarly covered, were arranged around the tureen. 'I'll be off now then, sir,' she said.

'Thanks, Mrs F. See you tomorrow.'

'She doesn't live in, then, your housekeeper?' Maddy couldn't help but ask.

'No, she lives with her feckless husband and a senile aunt. Do please sit down and we'll see what's in the dishes.'

'Mm, that smells good,' Maddy commented as Guy lifted a lid. She had been a bit worried that the food would be less than edible and the boys — well, Jamie, anyway — would be embarrassingly vociferous on the subject. 'What is it?'

'Looks like pot-roast pheasant,' said Guy. 'Better watch out for the pellets.'

'You mean you shot them?' asked Jamie, intrigued.

'My neighbour breeds them for shooting. I didn't personally shoot these.'

Maddy made a mental note. If a customer wanted game, she would know where to find it. She'd also have to find a recipe — it wasn't something she had cooked in Bournemouth.

'This is beautiful — game, chips and lots of vegetables. Isn't it, boys?'

'I didn't say she couldn't cook, but she sticks to the basics. Party food isn't her forte.'

'Well, I wouldn't like to tread on her toes.'

'She won't mind in the slightest if you do the catering for a church do. As I said, she's never done it. I've always bought in. Will you have some more, Jamie?'

Both boys managed a generous second helping, after which Guy moved the cheese board and fruit bowl from the sideboard to the table.

'I tend to stick to good old cheddar and stilton,' Guy explained. 'Is that okay?'

'Our favourites,' Hugo told him. 'Bath Olivers, too. Great!'

Maddy couldn't remember when she had last enjoyed someone else's food so much, she thought as she peeled a tangerine.

'Coffee, everyone?' asked Guy.

'Not for me,' the boys replied in unison.

'There's a pool table across the hall if you fancy a game, while your mother and I talk boring old church dos.' They needed no further invitation.

Maddy started to load everything onto the trolley. 'You don't have to do that,' said Guy.

'Force of habit,' she replied, continuing.

Guy joined in and they had soon cleared the table, whereupon he wheeled the trolley out of the dining room. Maddy followed him to a vast kitchen which, unlike the dining room, was ultra modern, equipped with state-of-the-art appliances.

'This is fabulous!' she exclaimed. 'I love the green Aga, but where's the dishwasher hiding?'

Guy laughed. 'It's right here.' He pulled open one of many identical doors. 'Look, you don't need . . . '

'Tell you what, why don't you make the coffee and I'll sort this lot out?'

'Deal!'

★　★　★

'It's been useful getting the lie of the land, so to speak, for your church do,' she told him as he set a coffee pot on the kitchen table. 'How much of the house do you use for the party?'

'Most of the ground floor. I keep the study locked. Drinks will be served in the hall, on production of a ticket. Someone will be there selling raffle tickets, too. There'll be nibbles on side tables but the main buffet-type feast will be in the dining room. Puddings and cheese will be brought in from the kitchen later.'

She took a seat at the table. 'Suppose you give me a list of anything you particularly like and I'll come up with a menu?'

'Sounds excellent. Black coffee?'

'Oh yes, please.'

'Brandy?'

'Better not.' She had had a glass and a bit of some excellent red wine and that was enough for her. 'Oh!'

'What is it?'

'Nothing, I hope. You know the expression about someone walking over your grave? Well, it felt like that — like a shadow drifting across my inner vision. Too much red wine,' she laughed.

'Are you sure you're all right?' He took the seat directly opposite and leaned forward, bringing him rather too close for comfort. God, he was attractive. 'You've gone quite pale.'

'I'm fine. I was just being silly.'

At which point her mobile phone shrilled into the quiet kitchen.

7

'Madeleine Leighton?'

'Speaking.'

Her quick intake of breath brought Guy's head round sharply. She turned away, the better to concentrate.

'No! What happened? . . . Oh my God! Yes, of course, right away . . . Yes, I'll find it.' She switched off and shrank down onto her chair.

'What is it, Maddy'

'It's Dawn. She's in Poole Hospital. They think she's taken something . . . '

'Come on. Let's go.'

'Wh-what?'

Her child was in hospital and this man wanted her to go somewhere with him.

'I mean I'll drive you to the hospital.'

'Oh! Are you sure? I mean, well, sorry, but how much have you had to drink?'

'Very little! A good thing you declined the brandy, otherwise I might have had a large one. Let's get going.'

As it was, she seemed to have been robbed of rational thought by a combination of the glass or so of wine she had had with dinner and the shocking news she had just received.

'I'll get the boys.'

'Wouldn't it be better if they stayed here?'

But Hugo had other ideas. 'I'd rather come with you, Mum,' he said.

'I doubt they'll let anyone in except your mother,' Guy told him gently. 'I'll look after her.'

'But . . .'

'I know how protective you feel towards Maddy, and that's good, but right now it might be better if you held the fort and looked after Jamie.'

He was rewarded by a long, studied look from Hugo. 'Very well, but you will keep us informed, won't you?'

'Of course. I'll drop you off at your

place on the way.'

So they all piled into Guy's sleek Jaguar, dropped the boys off at home, and were soon nudging the speed limit down the dual carriageway to Bere Regis and on to Poole.

'What were the twins doing this evening? I thought they were visiting a friend,' said Guy.

'That was the original plan, but Stacey wanted to go to an under-eighteen disco.'

'Have they been before?'

'No. Stacey's been, with her cousin, but I wouldn't let the twins go until they were fifteen. Oh, why must Dawn do something so stupid?'

'God knows. Peer pressure, perhaps. What about Sophie?'

'Sophie's the sensible one. Dawn's impulsive and inclined to be wild without Sophie's influence. It didn't protect her this time, though, did it?'

★   ★   ★

When they arrived a distraught Sophie was pacing the corridor of the intensive care unit. Dawn, visible through a doorway, lay unconscious in a single room. A frightening array of wires connected her to some impressive-looking equipment.

'Mummy!' Sophie hurled herself at Maddy, sobbing inconsolably.

Maddy held her close while peering through to where Dawn could be seen lying unconscious while a doctor and nurse adjusted various knobs and connections.

'What happened, love?'

Sophie sobbed more loudly. The doctor came out of the ward, looking severe. 'Are you the parents?'

'I'm her mother,' Maddy informed him. 'Guy is a neighbour . . . friend.'

'Dr Alexander.'

'What's happened to my daughter?'

'As far as we can gather, she took some vile substance at a disco, which had the predictable disastrous effects.'

'Oh Mum, I'm so sorry.'

'You don't have to be sorry, darling. I mean, *you* didn't give her anything, did you?'

'Of course not, but I should have looked after her.'

'I'll be having words with Penny.'

'Oh Mum, it wasn't Stacey who gave her something. It was her cousin, Cassandra.'

'And where are Cassandra and Stacey? And where is Penny?'

Sophie shrugged helplessly.

'How did it happen?'

'Well, Dawn and Cassandra went off to the ladies' together. They were ages in there. I was about to go in and find out if they were all right when they came out. They were both giggly but Dawn started to act strangely. She was really hyper, skipping onto the dance floor and throwing herself about like a wild thing. She looked feverish, too. Her face was very red and she was sweating profusely.

'The cousin got all stressed. She was dancing crazily, too, but she wasn't totally out of control like Dawn. She must have realised what was happening. Eventually she pulled Dawn off the floor, swearing at her — I didn't understand why at the time. She told her to drink plenty of water, which she did, but it didn't make any difference.'

The doctor had been listening to all this intently.

'Typical reaction to 'e's,' he said. 'Don't know why they do it. That particular disco is usually very responsible. What happened next, Sophie?'

'We all helped her outside to cool down and that was when she collapsed. I didn't know what to do, Mum.'

'Of course you didn't,' said Guy. 'Come on, let's go in and sit with her, talk to her — if that's all right, Doctor?'

'It's all you can do. That and pray, if you're so inclined.'

Maddy paused in the doorway, frozen with horror, seeing her child lying there unable to communicate. Sophie took her hand. 'Come on, Mum. Come and sit by the bed.'

Guy put an arm round her, gently squeezing her shoulder. 'Go on, Maddy,' he said gently, his deep voice soft and reassuring. 'I'm right behind you.'

'Thanks, Guy,' said Sophie. 'I'll get another chair.'

'Is it all right if I stay?' Guy asked the nurse who was busy in a corner but obviously ready to act if need be.

'It's supposed to be two visitors at a time, but in the circumstances we'll turn a blind eye. Use the hand gel, though, and put on one of the aprons.'

She indicated the bag of aprons hanging on the wall, pink plastic ones.

'Not sure it's my colour,' said Guy in a feeble attempt at humour.

Maddy leaned over and kissed Dawn's cheek, negotiating a space between the tubes to her nose and mouth. 'What are we going to do with you?' she asked. 'You're such a naughty girl. Why can't you be sensible like your sister?'

'That would be boring,' said Sophie.

'Right now, I'd settle for boring.'

The doctor reappeared at that moment.

'What's the prognosis, doctor?' asked Guy.

'She's a very sick young lady. Mind you, I've seen worse.' He was taking readings and adjusting equipment while he spoke. 'There's not much point in all of you staying. Why not go home and get some sleep?'

'I'm not leaving her,' said Maddy, 'but I think you should go home with Guy, Sophie, and tell the boys what's happening.'

'I want to stay.'

'Wouldn't you rather be alert when she comes round? Which could be as soon as tomorrow,' asked the doctor.

'Could it really? Oh Dawn, I'm so cross with you,' she told her unconscious twin. 'Why did you have to be so stupid?' She hugged Dawn as best she could. 'I suppose we might as well go, then, Guy.'

'I'll just get your mother a coffee

before we leave. Do you want anything to eat, Maddy?'

'I couldn't eat a thing, thanks. I feel a bit queasy, to be honest. Oh, not because of that lovely meal; more to do with this. But a coffee would be nice. That's very kind of you, Guy.'

After they'd left, Maddy felt abandoned. She chatted with the nurse from time to time and both nurse and doctor checked regularly on Dawn.

Despite the coffee and her will to stay awake, Maddy nodded off in the armchair beside the bed. In the early hours she jerked upright, woken by a small sound from the bed.

'Dawn? I'm here, darling. Mummy's here.'

'Mummy, I feel . . . '

The nurse who had remained in the room all night moved swiftly over with a kidney dish but too late to catch the copious flow of vomit from Dawn.

'Oh, I'm sorry,' Dawn sobbed. 'I feel terrible. My head's splitting.'

Dr Alexander walked in. 'Ah, you're awake. That's good. You had us all worried.'

'I'm sorry. My head hurts so much.'

'We'll give you something for the headache. You're lucky to be alive, do you realise?'

'What about . . . ?'

'If you're going to ask about Stacey's cousin, then she's all right,' Maddy informed her tersely. 'I'm very cross with her, though.'

'With all due respect,' said Dr Alexander, 'it's entirely up to the individual to decide whether or not to take drugs if they're offered. Your daughter's had a bad reaction, probably drank copious amounts of water to counteract the heat and thirst and, in so doing, overloaded the kidneys. Am I right, Dawn?'

'I thought it was the best thing to do. So did Stacey. They all told me to drink plenty.'

'Yes, well that's a bit of a misconception. You should certainly drink around a pint an hour to counteract dehydration, but more than that and the blood becomes diluted, the plasma sodium levels drop and the kidneys can't cope. The brain can sometimes swell, too. You're lucky. Yours didn't.'

'I didn't know.'

'Well, you do now.'

'I'll never touch drugs again.'

'At least you'll know what to do next time.'

'There won't be a next time.'

'What you need now is a pot of weak tea and a good rest.'

'Can I go home?'

'I'd like to keep you in overnight; the rest of the night, that is. You've been on a saline drip to build up the sodium levels in your blood. We'll continue to monitor you for the next few hours and then, if you're all right, you can go home. But you must rest. We need the bed for someone who is really ill, and not with something self-inflicted. If you're all right by lunchtime tomorrow, you can go.'

'Oh God, I feel so ashamed.'

'Right, well, that's enough apologies. Just be sensible in future.'

'I shall, I shall, I promise.'

'Good. Well, I'm going off duty shortly and I sincerely hope not to see you again for the same reason. You gave your mum and sister quite a fright.'

'Yes, and thank you, Doctor.'

'Thank you, indeed,' added Maddy. 'Oh, here comes your tea.'

With the wires disconnected, Dawn drank the tea, after which she was moved to another ward where she settled down for a sleep.

'You might as well get some rest too, Mrs Leighton,' the nurse suggested. 'You can go home when the trains start running and give us a ring at lunchtime.'

Somewhat reassured by Dawn's improvement, Maddy spent the next few hours slumped uncomfortably in the armchair beside the bed. She was woken at six by a nurse bringing her tea and toast. Dawn was still asleep as she crept out to make her way home by taxi and train.

*　*　*

The following day, after checking that Dawn was allowed to leave the hospital, Guy offered to drive Maddy and Sophie, who insisted on coming along, to pick her up.

'Just in case you're planning on getting all weepy,' he told Maddy wryly, 'and can't see to drive.'

'We'll miss the church service this afternoon,' said Maddy. 'Aren't you a churchwarden or something?'

'For my sins, yes, but I'm not indispensable.'

*　*　*

Sophie was shocked by Dawn's appearance. She rushed to where she was sitting, her packed bag on the floor at her feet, and clasped her in a bear hug.

'Darling, you look awful!' she cried.

'Thanks, Sophe. You look pretty grim yourself.'

'From not sleeping, worrying about you.'

'Sorry.'

'Come on then, you two,' said Maddy. 'Guy's waiting in the car, in a taxi lane or something. The car park's miles away, too far for Dawn to walk, anyway.'

When they reached the car, Guy was talking through his open window to a traffic warden. 'Oh look, here they come now,' he was saying with his most charming smile. 'Thank you very much, my dear.'

The warden, a fleshy-faced blonde in her forties, beamed with pleasure. 'You've got a very caring dad,' she told them.

Maddy could see Dawn about to disabuse the woman, which would not have been a good idea. 'You two get in the back,' she said sharply, adding quietly, 'We're not supposed to be parked here. Thank you,' she tacked on for the warden.

Guy pulled away. In the back Dawn leaned forward. 'You're not my dad,' she said with some of her old spirit.

'No, I'm not. If I were, I'd be keeping a very close eye on you from now on.'

'Well, you're not, and he's not here, nor would he care if he were.'

'What does he think about all this?' he asked Maddy quietly.

'You haven't told him?' Dawn asked, appalled.

'I haven't, but maybe I should.'

'You should,' said Guy. 'You shouldn't have to bear all the worry and responsibility for your family alone.'

'I'm getting used to it, but maybe he should know what's going on.' Maddy could hear Dawn sniffling in the back but went on anyway. 'I mean, suppose the outcome had been different, Dawn? Suppose you hadn't recovered?'

'But I did. It's got nothing to do with him. I've already said I won't do it again.'

'You won't,' Maddy agreed. 'No more under-eighteen discos for you, I'm afraid. You can stay with Stacey occasionally, but not if her cousin's there.'

'Okay.'

'And . . . '

'I said okay!'

'Dawn.' Guy spoke sternly, making eye contact through the rear-view mirror.

'Sorry, Mum, this headache's getting worse.'

'Oh darling, why didn't you say?'

For reply, Dawn settled against her twin and closed her eyes.

8

After that, life took on a routine of sorts. Workmen continued to come and go. The main house was newly wired, the bathrooms finished. The extension Maddy had decided on, approved by the planning department, was almost complete. There was still some decorating to be done, but the place was beginning to feel like home.

Carpets were duly fitted and curtains hung. Maddy then sorted through the furniture in storage and had some chosen pieces delivered to their new home. The rest went to the local sale room. It was quite unintentional but most of the latter, she realised, had been more Rob's choice than hers; pieces she had never really liked but to which she had given house room to keep the peace.

The church do at the manor was

coming up and Maddy decided it was time to mend fences with Penny and Stacey. Dawn had survived after all, and she seemed to have grown up overnight. Sophie had changed, too. She seemed more mature and outgoing.

'Penny,' Maddy began after the usual greetings. Penny sounded flustered and Maddy wondered if she had interrupted something. 'I was wondering if you'd all like to come to a buffet supper at a neighbour's house on Saturday in aid of church funds.'

'Wow! That sounds a bit heavy.'

'It won't be anything of the sort. Thing is, I've been persuaded to do the catering for the event, so it's a bit of a tryout, and I could do with some friendly support . . . '

'Oh, er, in that case we'd love to come. What time, and how do we get there?'

'I'll send you a map. Oh Penny, I'm so glad you're coming. I need a friend. I was feeling a bit nervous. In a way, it will showcase my catering business.'

'How's that going?'

'Slowly. I'm getting small commissions — parties, special-occasion cakes, that sort of thing. But that's about to change.'

'How come?'

'My sister-in-law . . . '

'The redoubtable Liz?'

'Yes, Liz. She's been wonderful since Rob took off with his floozie.'

'Probably feels guilty on his behalf.'

'Anyway, she sees things on a broader scale and wants me to get proper premises and start producing high-quality ready meals.'

'Is that what you want to do, Maddy? I mean, I can't see you as a businesswoman.'

'I think basically it's an excellent idea. I'm negotiating right now for premises on a new industrial estate that's not far away, and I've already decided on some of the dishes.'

'That sounds positive. I almost wish Gerry would take off with his PA.'

'Not much chance of that,' Maddy

laughed, thinking of the bespectacled grey-haired lady who had worked for and adored Gerry, and his father before him, for decades.

'Well no, I know, but I do rather envy you the excitement of a whole new life, doing something completely different.'

'Yes it is exciting, I suppose, but it's also quite terrifying at times. I'm completely responsible for the family now, financially and in every other way.'

'Sounds like you're doing a great job,' Penny said dismissively. 'Look, I've got to go, but do send me that map.'

'Will do, and it's been nice talking to you. Bye.'

Perhaps Penny was rather more envious than she had let on. She had sounded cool and distant, decidedly odd. Perhaps their friendship had run its course now they no longer lived within a stone's throw of each other. Perhaps it had been a bad idea inviting them.

Her new life, though. Was it exciting? Yes, she supposed it was. She may have been forced out of the comfort zone of her old life, but she was by no means undaunted about her future prospects. She was *not*. What kept her going? Was it a determination to show Rob she could manage without him? Was it a dormant desire to do something other than run a home? Or was it the inspiration of living here among the green hills and fresh air of the Dorset countryside, away from the polluted streets of town?

Obviously it was a combination of all three. Of course there were problems and responsibilities, of a kind she had never dealt with before, but it *was* exciting. Looking back, Rob's input had been mainly negative. Whether she had been making suggestions to do with furnishings, schools, holidays, whatever, his immediate reaction had been negative. Everything had been met with a putdown, maybe calculated, maybe not, but the apparent intention had been to put her in her place and make her aware of who was boss. If their marriage had been childless, she sometimes wondered if they would have stayed together. She very much doubted it.

She wondered briefly how Rob was coping with his new life; how he was getting on with Holly. Holly would not be put down easily. Had he found work over there? She wondered about it for a while but then, remembering the heartless way he had ended their marriage, she realised she didn't actually care.

Saturday would be her big test — the night of the cheese and wine do in aid of church funds. She would be showcasing her talents, but not only that, she realised: she wanted to impress Guy, for whatever reason.

The next few days she spent cooking and freezing — terrines and pâtés, vegetarian quiches, quiches with bacon, dips like hummus and guacamole; and for puddings, chocolate torte, tarte au citron, pavlovas and tiny choux buns for the tower she planned to build. She would buy bread from that dear little shop with the funny name in Dorchester, and salads and fruit for the fruit salad from that greengrocer who sold local farm produce alongside more exotic produce.

On Friday night Maddy went over and over her plans for the party, staying awake until the small hours. But come the dawn, she woke full of energy and raring to go.

She loved this peaceful start to the day, enjoying a cup of tea in the quiet kitchen to the sound of the countryside waking up. It wasn't yet light, but soon there would be the sound of birdsong as the feathered creatures laid claim to their territory. A couple of tractors rumbled by. She regretted her ignorance about farm work in the different seasons. Were they collecting crops, planting winter wheat? Or what?

It wasn't long before the sounds of the family coming to life shut out other sounds. Water gurgled from showers and flushes. Thank goodness they had plenty of bathrooms and didn't have to fight over them. One by one they appeared, by which time Maddy had laid the table with cutlery, crockery and their usual choice of breakfast foods: cereals, juice, rolls, ham, cheese and fruit. Slices of wholemeal bread waited by the toaster. Bacon wouldn't be on the menu today. Breakfast would be strictly continental — they had a very busy day ahead.

* * *

'Are you going into town this morning?' Dawn asked, pressing the toaster slide.

'You know I am, Dawn. I have to pick up bread and salad stuff. Why?'

'Sophe and I would like to buy something to wear this evening. You know, something suitably nun-like for a church do, but with a bit of sparkle.'

'Sounds like a contradiction in terms,' Hugo put in. 'Sparkly nuns.'

'What would you know? Can we, Mum?'

'Of course, if you promise to help me

carry everything back to the car.'

'Deal!'

★　★　★

By mid-morning Maddy was getting impatient, concerned about how time was flying by. 'Look, girls, if you can't find something in this boutique we'll have to give up. You know I've got masses to do.'

'Sorry, Mum. Oh look, Dawn — how about something like this?'

They each managed to choose a sparkly tunic — Sophie's in cyclamen, Dawn's in jade — with just sufficient sparkle to please them, which they intended to wear with black leggings and ballerina pumps.

'Oh, what do you think of this, Sophe?' Dawn asked, stopping to finger a slim black sheath with a discreetly low neckline and jet bead decoration.

'I thought you were happy with your choice, Dawn,' said Maddy, exasperated. 'And it's a little too old for you, don't you think?'

'Not for me, Mum! For you!'

'Me?'

'You'd look fantastic in it.'

Maddy looked at the dress doubtfully. She didn't usually wear black, but it *was* elegant. Should she?

She was soon emerging from the fitting room, giving a twirl and a wiggle of her hips.

'Wow!' the girls exclaimed in unison. 'You look fantastic,' Sophie added.

Maddy studied her reflection thoughtfully. She was no longer a size ten, but she was lucky that her body had remained reasonably trim with no pads of fat to ruin the line of her clothes. The neckline revealed neat, firm cleavage — well supported, true, but not bad considering she had fed four babies, two of them twins. It would look really good with her push-up bra to 'lift and separate' as the ads claimed. With smart heels and simple gold jewellery she would certainly look the part of a successful businesswoman.

'It is nice, isn't it?' she conceded.

'Nice? It's absolutely bloody marvellous. You can't not buy it!'

'I agree,' said Sophie.

Maddy looked at the price ticket. 'It's very expensive,' she ventured.

Dawn looked at it, too. 'Cheap at the price,' she declared. 'You haven't bought anything for yourself for ages, Mum. Treat yourself.'

So she did. Together they humped their smart carriers back to the car along with bags of loaves and rolls from the baker's, and a couple of bags from the greengrocer bulging with salads and fruit.

'Leave all the food in the pantry,' she told them when they got home. 'Then you can take all your finery upstairs.' The excruciating sounds of Jamie on his new cello came from the music room. 'Oh God, is that a car?'

'Hi, Mum.' Hugo appeared from the hall. 'I think our guests have arrived. I'll put some coffee on. Did you buy any goodies to go with it?'

'Of course! Some of those lovely almond things. They're in the pantry with the bread for tonight. I'll just put the chicken casserole in the oven for lunch.'

By which time Penny had parked her car round the side of the house and was at the kitchen door. A little sign at the front directed all comers to the parking area and thence to the back door, once no doubt the tradesmen's entrance, an arrangement which seemed more friendly and which suited them.

'Maddy! What a super place! I'd no idea it was so grand!'

'You should have seen it when we took it. Do come in. No Tim?'

'No, sorry; he's off to Japan in the morning and wanted an early night.'

'Shame. Hugo, if you do the coffee, I'll show Penny and Stacey their room. Are you all right with a twin room?'

'Perfect.'

They followed Maddy, taking their overnight bags and chatting cheerfully as they went.

'Phew!' Jamie appeared in the kitchen. 'I'd forgotten what a yackbag Penny is. I might go and see if Dominic's home after lunch, escape for a game of tennis.'

Hugo laughed. 'She's pretty over-powering, isn't she?'

After coffee the young all retreated, leaving Penny and Maddy alone in the kitchen.

'I've never really apologised for what happened at that disco,' Penny began.

'Look, Penny, it wasn't your fault. Let's just draw a line under that little episode. However, I've told the twins they can come and stay when the cousin isn't there, but no more discos. I just want you to have a nice weekend with us. I'm not sure what to expect from this evening, but I'm quite looking forward to it.'

'And you're doing the catering?'

'I am. Scary, isn't it?'

'I'd be terrified, but it's what you do best.' A figure passed the window. 'My God! Don't look now but Mr Darcy is standing at your door.'

'What?'

Maddy laughed but as she looked towards the open kitchen door, Guy appeared, standing there looking suitably solemn and, truly Darcy-like, riding hat in one hand, crop in the other.

'Who is that?' Penny whispered.

'Hello, Guy. Come in. Come and meet Penny, a friend of mine from Bournemouth. She's come to lend me a bit of moral support.'

Guy nodded to Penny across the room. 'Nice to meet you, Penny. I've heard of you, of course.'

Damn, of course he had, Maddy realised with acute embarrassment — from the disco incident.

'Nothing good, I hope,' Penny simpered.

Penny was flirting. Maddy had never seen her acting like this before. Certainly Guy wasn't taking the bait but remained solemn and unsmiling. He turned his back on Penny so that only Maddy could see his expression as he gave her a long, slow wink.

She didn't know what to make of that. He was behaving to Penny as he had to her when they'd first met — not exactly unfriendly, but lacking warmth, certainly. Now he was winking at her as if they were fellow conspirators; as if they shared a secret to which Penny wasn't party, which sent pleasant little shivers down her spine.

'I came to see if you needed a hand, Maddy. I'll help you carry things across when you're ready.'

'It's okay, Guy. We'll bring everything over to your place mid-afternoon and stash everything we need to in your fridges.'

'Shall I come back to help?'

'I think we can manage, thanks.'

'See you later, Maddy.' And on a terser note: 'Penny.'

'Whew! Is he something!'

They watched through the kitchen window as he crossed to the gate where his horse was tied up — a tall, slim but broad-shouldered figure, his dark hair curling over his collar, the jodhpurs clinging to well-muscled thighs.

Maddy smiled, the thought of that wink giving her the shivers again. 'Guy's very nice,' she agreed.

'Nice? He's bloody gorgeous!'

'If you say so. G and T before lunch?'

'Now you're talking. There's some wine, by the way, in the back of my car.'

'We can have a glass with lunch. The wine for this evening is all laid on.'

The children all turned up as if by magic at five minutes to one and took their places around the long refectory table in the kitchen, where they usually ate. Any awkwardness about recent events was swept away as friendships were rekindled.

'We're going for a walk after lunch,' Maddy told them. 'Any of you want to come?'

'We'll come,' the girls volunteered.

'Jamie and I are going to help Robin clear leaves from the vicarage lawn,' said Hugo.

Jamie looked surprised but said nothing.

'You're becoming regular country folk,' Penny laughed. 'I can't wait to meet your other neighbours this evening.'

So long as she wasn't expecting them all to look like Guy, Maddy thought.

9

Refreshed after their walk, they set about transferring the food to the manor. Hugo and Jamie, summoned back from the vicarage by a call from Maddy, returned in time to help pack everything into the people carrier. Penny insisted on helping, so in the end she, Maddy and the girls all trouped over to Guy's. They stashed the food in the pantry and paused to look at the transformation that had taken place. Trestle tables had been set up in the hall and dining room, overlaid with white linen cloths, and plates stacked in readiness for the evening do.

'It looks stunning, Guy,' said Maddy. 'You have been working hard. And what fabulous flower arrangements!'

'Dom's been a great help arranging the tables,' Guy told her, 'but we can't claim responsibility for the flowers.

They're entirely down to Mrs F.'

'They look really professional.'

'Can I offer you all some tea?'

'No, thank you.' Maddy ignored Penny's scowl and went on: 'We won't hold you up, and we have to get ready ourselves. We'll be coming back early, though, to put food on tables.'

This brought the smile back to Penny's face. With the food dealt with for the time being and out of the way, they were able to concentrate on dressing up for the evening. By half past six they were all assembled downstairs and raring to go.

'Don't you all look gorgeous!' Penny exclaimed. She herself was wearing a silky purple trouser suit with a low-necked top and long, dangly earrings.

All three girls had donned their glamorous new tops. Stacey's was a bright sparkly bronze, similar in style and contrasting with the cyclamen and jade the twins had chosen. The boys were in crisp striped shirts with dark trousers but no ties. They all looked heart-breakingly young and vulnerable. Maddy again experienced regret and anger that Rob wasn't there to see them, quickly followed by a 'his loss, serves him right' thought.

'Shall we go?' she said.

'I thought it started at half past seven?' said Dawn.

'Not for the workers — that's us,' Maddy informed her.

'Not me — I'm a guest.'

'You don't have to come yet, but if you don't, you'll have to make your own way over on foot. I expect we can manage with Guy and Dominic's help.'

'Well, I'm coming with you,' said Penny.

'Me, too. I want to check out the local talent,' said Stacey.

In the end, they all piled into the people carrier.

There was something of an altercation going on when they arrived. Maddy tucked the car away in a corner of the courtyard and they all clambered out somewhat uncertainly.

Dominic approached from the direction of the stables, muddy and unkempt, with an angry Guy berating him, doubtless reminding him of the houseful of guests they were expecting shortly.

'Sorry, Dad. I lost track of time.' He removed his helmet to reveal a head of thick, dark hair just like his father's. 'My watch seems to have stopped.'

'Tag Heuer watches don't stop.'

'It was from the chanteuse,' Dominic replied mockingly. 'So it's probably a fake.'

Guy made an impatient noise. 'Get out of my sight, and don't come down till you look and smell respectable.'

'I'll be out of your hair soon enough,' Dominic muttered, disappearing into the house but not before pulling a face behind his father's back as Guy turned to greet them.

'Sorry about that,' he apologised. 'Come in, all of you.'

They followed him through to the hall. Bottles and glasses were neatly lined up on the first table. Others held dishes of nibbles. Candles in silver candlesticks stood centrally, as yet unlit, on each table. One which had three branches had been lit, its flames reflecting softly in the polished wood panelling of the hall.

'My, Mrs Frimley has been busy, polishing all this wood,' said Maddy.

'Actually, I did it. Mrs F. has enough to do. She arranged the flowers, as I told you, and she also made a couple of corn dollies for some reason. Well, it is autumn.'

'I'm impressed. It all looks lovely, Guy.' Maddy admired the beautifully arranged vases of flowers on every available surface. 'Why don't you have a drink while Penny and I take over?'

The tension visibly went out of him. 'That's the best offer I've had all day. What about you kids? Do you want to go off and play billiards or something?'

'We're doing the waitressing,' Sophie informed him. 'We'll help Mum in the kitchen for now.'

'That makes us males superfluous,' Hugo declared.

'Don't be too sure,' Guy laughed, his good humour restored.

'May I ask what Dom was talking about — being out of your hair?' Hugo asked Guy.

'He wants to go off travelling.'

'Really?'

'Really,' Guy replied darkly. 'As you see, he sometimes has his scattier moments. How on earth will he cope abroad on his own? Now then, if you don't mind you can help Dominic carry some chairs through from the store-room before you disappear. The oldies always want to sit around and gossip at these dos.'

Dominic appeared on cue, showered and shaved, wearing a jazzy waistcoat over a frilled evening shirt.

'Very smart,' said Guy. 'That shirt looks familiar.'

'Well, as you wanted me to make an effort . . .'

'You thought you'd borrow one of mine.'

'You don't mind?'

'Of course not.' He gave his son a playful punch. 'I may return the compliment one day. Don't get it dirty carrying the chairs.'

'What chairs?'

While the boys set about their allotted task, Maddy led the way to the kitchen.

'Mm, you seem to know your way around Guy's kitchen,' Penny commented snidely.

'Penny! I loaded the dishwasher after we'd all had dinner here last week — to discuss this very event.'

'You don't have to explain. You're a free agent now.'

'Almost. I've applied for my decree nisi with the help of my solicitor. It'll be another six weeks before I can get the decree absolute.'

'You're as good as free, then.'

'All the same, I wouldn't like you to get the wrong idea.'

'Or the right one. Okay, okay. Sorry.'

'Right, let's get down to work. There are platters of food in the fridges, all cling-filmed and ready to put out. You can put them out now but leave the film on to cover them till the last moment. I'm going to wash a few dishes for salads. They're freshly washed and in bags. The terrines and pâtés must go out at the last minute. We don't want to give anyone food poisoning.'

By a quarter past seven the tables were arranged and they all congregated in the drawing room.

'Fabulous room — shabby, though,' Penny muttered softly.

'I just want a word with the girls,' Maddy said.

'It's okay, Mum. We know — one glass of wine, and then mineral water.'

'Good. So long as you remember.'

'We will. Right now, all I want is a lemonade.'

'Here we are, ladies.' Guy came in carrying two glasses of red wine, handing one to Maddy, the other to

Penny. 'I've opened a few bottles of red and a couple of white. The rest of the white is in the drinks fridge. I don't think there'll be a shortage of volunteer barmen. The lemonade's in the kitchen, girls.'

'Are the guests allowed to drink free booze all night?' Penny asked curiously.

'No, it's one glass and free food with the ticket. After that there's a charge for drinks — don't forget, it's in aid of church funds, so we need to make some money. Also, we don't want to turn out a load of drunken drivers at the end of the evening. I've put a little notice up, so there'll be no ambiguity about the charge.'

Guests began to arrive. Coats were stashed in the cloakroom and drinks dispensed by Dominic and Hugo.

'A word, boys,' said Guy as a large red-faced man in a tweed suit walked in. By his side was a diminutive grey-haired lady elegantly clad in a black suit with an artfully arranged emerald scarf to match the whopping

234

stones in her platinum rings. Maddy, who was standing nearby, listened curiously. 'After his first drink, start to water his wine.'

Maddy was all ears now, shocked.

'Understood, Dad.'

'What was that about?' Maddy asked. 'You can't do that, surely?'

'Colonel Ashworth *will* insist on driving that great bus of his,' Guy explained quietly. 'It's a vintage Bentley of which he's inordinately proud. He's the world's worst driver, unfortunately, and expects everyone to get out of his way. After a few drinks, he's practically lethal.'

'Sounds like he shouldn't be driving at all. Can't you confiscate his keys and order a taxi?'

'We'll see. That could be plan B. I sometimes think his slurred speech is more of an affectation than anything.'

People were piling in now. The rest of the food was brought out and covers removed. Maddy couldn't help but be delighted by the comments she heard.

'Brilliant effort,' said Robin, who appeared at her elbow, drink in hand.

'Thanks, Robin. This is Penny, by the way, a friend from Bournemouth. Penny, Robin, our vicar.'

'Goodness, I thought it was only policemen who were getting younger. Very nice to meet you, Robin.'

Stacey sidled up. 'Hi,' she greeted him, and told him her name.

'My daughter, Stacey, Robin. Stacey, this is Robin, the local vicar.'

'How nice.' She smiled sweetly and promptly sidled away.

'Was it something I said?' He grinned.

'Can I get you something?' Maddy asked a group of elderly ladies who, as Guy had predicted, were sitting in a group, gossiping.

'I'm all right,' one lady assured her, 'but I think Edie might like a lemonade.'

'Sure. I'll get some.'

'That pâté's scrumptious. Do you know where Guy bought it?'

Maddy smiled. 'Actually, I've done the catering for this evening, so yours truly made it.'

'Oh, very nice, dear. Did you hear that, Edie?' Then in a stage whisper: 'Edie's a bit hard of hearing. She's the oldest.'

'We're all sisters,' another volunteered.

'How wonderful!'

Maddy extricated herself as soon as she could from the amazing quintet of sisters, the youngest of whom was seventy-eight, she was informed, and brought them lemonade before moving on to circulate and socialise. She noted that Penny was making the most of coming without Tim, flirting with all and sundry, and vaguely hoped she wouldn't be lumped in with Penny as 'those tarty Bournemouth birds'.

As she went into the drawing room she thought how beautiful, romantic even, it looked by candlelight. The antique furniture had been waxed within an inch of its life. The drapes and magnificent oriental carpet might be shabby and worn, but the wall sconces softened imperfections and revealed only innate quality. Shabby chic, perhaps. A group parted and she was able to see the tall, elegant figure of Guy, his shoulders broad, his dark hair curling Darcy-fashion over his collar. She caught her breath as a stab of something not altogether unwelcome but slightly alarming shot through her. She was about to return to the more familiar ground of the kitchen when Guy turned and looked straight at her. Had he read her thoughts? He started towards her, his dark eyes unfathomable in the soft light.

'Hi, Maddy. Are you enjoying yourself?'

'Very much so, Guy.'

'No, you're not. What you're doing is scurrying round, looking after everyone else. Now — ' He took her elbow and led her from the room. ' — what you are going to do is sit down with a drink and a plateful of food, and think of yourself for once.'

'Yessir,' she replied mockingly.

'And I'm going to do the same.' With which he pushed her gently towards the dining room. 'You've really done us proud,' he told her. 'Everything looks delicious. I need a tray, not a plate.'

'Try the duck terrine, and I see the filou parcels have been largely ignored. These are vegetarian and these, chicken and bacon.'

He picked up one of the latter and took a bite. As it started to crumble he stuffed the whole thing in, trying not to laugh with his mouth full.

'You should have warned me,' he said once he had swallowed.

'You should use your plate and not be so hasty.'

'Yes, ma'am.'

He led her, each carrying a laden plate and glass of wine, to a small sitting room which happened to be empty. 'I suppose keeping the door closed must have kept people out,' he said. 'Let's sit here.'

'Here' was a two-seater settee with a low table conveniently placed in front of it. Maddy tried not to lean forwards as she sat, suddenly aware that her neckline was lower than she usually wore. She tried to sit nearer the arm than the middle of the settee but Guy appeared not to notice her attack of self-consciousness and sat comfortably on the other half, his thigh just touching hers.

'I can honestly say we've never had such delicious food at any of our church dos,' he assured her. 'You may well get a regular commission from future hosts.'

'I don't mind. I could probably offer cut-price rates,' she joked.

'Well, you certainly couldn't do it for nothing. It's your job, don't forget.'

'It's hard to forget. On Monday I'm going to look at a unit on the new industrial estate to see if it's suitable for cooking and packaging ready meals, though I'm not sure it's what I want to do.'

'Is that sister-in-law of yours going with you?'

'No, she can't, but I know what she'd say. She's always so positive. She'd be sure to say go for it. Deal with the problems later.' She laughed nervously, and looked up when he didn't speak.

'Is that what you think, Maddy?'

'I'm not exactly sure.'

'I'd be inclined to take the same line as Liz unless there were glaring reasons against it, such as your not really wanting to go down that route, or if there were some smelly industry next door which might taint the food.'

'I never thought of that.'

'Would — er — would you like me to come with you?'

'Well, yes, if you can spare the time. It would be useful to have a second opinion.' And no one would pressure her, she couldn't help but think, even in the twenty-first century, if she had a man in tow.

'That's settled, then.'

'Are you sure? I mean, don't you

241

have things to do?'

'Nothing I can't reschedule. Is that a date, then?'

She laughed then — a funny kind of date. 'It is. Would you like pudding or cheese?'

'I don't know if I can find room for any more food, but I'm willing to try.'

'Oh, there you are, Mum.' Dawn appeared from the dining room at the same time as Maddy and Guy emerged into the hall.

'How's it going? We've only just managed to grab some food.'

'And delicious it was,' said Guy. 'We're foraging for pudding now.'

'They're going fast. We put them out a little while ago.'

'Oh, is there anything left?'

'Don't worry, we kept one of the raspberry pavlovas back.'

'Good girl. That all right for you, Guy?'

'My favourite.'

'Just as well. The choux bun tower seems to have collapsed. There's some fruit salad left, but the interesting bits have been picked out — mainly by the boys.'

People were beginning to drift off.

'Great party, Guy.'

'Fabulous food.'

'See you in church.'

'I'm driving,' declared one stalwart lady as her husband staggered uncertainly towards their parked car, and Maddy and Guy watched through the open door.

'Fine by me,' he replied, as she opened the passenger door for him to collapse into the seat.

'Oh, I've just remembered. What about the colonel and his lady? Are they still here?' Guy asked as Dominic appeared beside them.

''Fraid so, and he's rather the worse for wear in spite of the watered drinks,' the younger man replied.

'Right. Come on. I'll drive his car home and you can follow, then drive us back. I'll get his keys from his jacket which is hanging in the hall.'

'Are you sure?'

'Now would be favourite. Come on!'

Having obtained the keys, they hurried out and round the house to where the cars were parked. Soon two cars could be heard being started up and driven off.

'What's going on?' Penny enquired, coming out of the drawing room. 'The old army type thought he could hear his car being driven away.'

'Would you mind keeping him occupied, Penny? Offer him a cognac. I know Guy's got some somewhere.' She remembered the dinner party which had ended with that alarming phone call when they never got round to having a brandy. 'I'll find it. Just keep him happy and here for the next fifteen minutes.'

Maddy dug out some brandy balloons and found Guy's best cognac. She poured some into two of the glasses and looked up as Penny returned.

'His wife's not too happy with the offer,' Penny informed her, 'but the colonel's delighted.'

'I'll take them in.'

The colonel's wife was pacing the floor, looking worried. 'I really think we should go, dear.'

'And so we shall, precious. You wouldn't deny a man a decent cognac, would you?'

'Here we are,' said Maddy, handing the larger amount to the colonel, still seated beside the fire as if he had taken root. 'Don't worry, Mrs Wentworth — we'll see you get home safely,' she assured her quietly.

'I don't see how you can do that,' came the querulous reply.

'Guy's got a plan,' Maddy whispered.

The colonel was still sitting there when Guy and Dominic returned.

'Having a good time, colonel?' Guy enquired, with a wink for Maddy.

'Splendid, my boy. Superb cognac.'

'I do think we should leave soon,' said his wife.

'I'm ready when you are,' said the colonel, draining his glass and pushing himself up with surprising agility.

'I think he may not have drunk too much after all,' Maddy said to Guy as she followed him from the room.

'Better safe than sorry.'

'Let me get your coats,' said Maddy as the colonel and his wife followed them into the hall. Once they were snugly buttoned up, Guy opened the front door and they all moved onto the porch.

'Thought I parked the car over there,' said the colonel.

'Ah, I think someone must have driven it home for you.'

'Wh-what? If there's any damage to the old bus . . . '

'Come on, I'll take you in my car and you can find out for yourself,' said Guy.

The colonel's wife walked round the Jaguar and ran her hand over the bonnet, which was still warm. 'Thanks, Guy,' she said quietly.

He said nothing, just smiled in reply. 'Back in twenty minutes,' he told them.

'So that's how they do things in the

country,' said Penny.

'What do you mean?'

'No fuss, just quietly caring for each other.'

'Yes. It's lovely, isn't it? I'm going to make a start on clearing up.'

Some of the female guests had had the same idea and together they made short shrift of clearing the tables and carrying things out to the kitchen.

'You're not to do the dishes,' Mrs Frimley told Maddy. 'I can finish off in the morning. You've done enough, and it's been a real treat to have such nice food.'

'Thank you, Mrs F. I may put another load in the dishwasher before I go. You've made a wonderful job of the tables and flowers, by the way. It all looks fantastic.'

'Any time, dear. I'm off home now. I'll be back tomorrow.'

Guy returned in time to say goodbye to her and the other helpers. 'We must work out some figures before we forget,' he said to Maddy. Sophie yawned. 'Oh,

I can see you're missing your beauty sleep. Penny, can you drive the people carrier?'

'It's the same model as ours, so yes,' she replied uncertainly.

'Would you mind driving everyone home while Maddy and I discuss business?'

'No problem.' She gave Maddy a knowing smirk before they all crowded into the Previa and whooshed out into the cold night. Suddenly the house was quiet.

'I'm off to bed,' Dominic announced, appearing from the billiard room.

'See you tomorrow, Dom. Thanks for your help.'

Maddy followed Guy into the kitchen where the table had been cleared and wiped down.

'Would you like a coffee?' he asked.

'No thanks, not this late — it keeps me awake and I'd like to sleep tonight.'

'Just a cognac, then. We can't keep it all for the colonel.'

She laughed. Tiredness had suddenly

hit her, together with a feeling of suppressed excitement. *Remember your age*, she told herself.

'We might as well enjoy it in comfort. Let's go into the drawing room.'

He placed two crystal balloons of cognac on coasters on a low polished table, gesturing to Maddy to sit on the buttoned velvet chesterfield behind it. As he sat beside her, she picked up her glass — as a defence? she asked herself, for that would presume that his thoughts were running parallel to her own.

He took a draught from his glass, replaced it on the table and, removing hers from shaking fingers, placed it beside his own. His fingers lightly encircled her wrist and she looked up at him. His eyes looked darker than usual and she feared that her own reflected the enlarged pupils that suggested arousal — or maybe it was the soft lighting in the room.

'Maddy,' he said softly, 'I should have said this earlier: you look absolutely beautiful tonight.'

She met his gaze, startled. His hold on her wrist was barely discernible. 'Thank you,' she muttered eventually.

'Thank you for being a superb co-host,' he said with a smile.

'I thought I was the hired help.'

'Far from it.' His free arm moved to encircle her shoulders, and his clasping fingers slid up to her upper arm, drawing her towards him. 'I've been wanting to do this all evening,' he murmured, and his head lowered to hers, his lips pressing gently, tentatively, on hers.

I mustn't, I mustn't, she told herself silently, but the temptation was too strong, he was far too attractive, and her arms moved of their own volition — one sliding round his back to hold him closer, the fingers of her freed hand stroking up his neck into the dark hair thickly curling at his nape. This, though she didn't say as much, was something she had wanted to do all evening and on several other occasions.

As she felt the soft velvet under her

back and his weight half covering her body, she closed her eyes and gave herself up to the pleasure of his embrace, aware that her body was moving invitingly against his, her legs parting to allow one of his to settle between.

A sound, irritating and increasingly shrill, inserted itself into this crazy dreamland where pleasure reigned supreme.

'Oh God, it's my phone,' she gasped, struggling to sit up.

Guy, as bleary-eyed and confused as Maddy felt, sat up, running a hand through his hair.

'Sorry,' she said, swinging her legs to the floor and standing up, at the same time pulling down her skirt which had ridden up, revealing the lacy tops of her 'stay-up' stockings and probably her flimsy French knickers, too.

She retrieved her phone from her bag in the hall. 'Rob?' she said, seeing the caller identity, astonished and furious at the same time.

251

'Yes, my sweet. Your husband, remember?'

'My ex-husband, just about. What do you want, Rob?'

'Just wondering how you're doing. Did you get a good price for the house?'

'I don't see that that's any of your business. I could ask the same about the agency share you sold.'

'Thing is, it's expensive renting and almost impossible to set up the same type of business here, in the foreseeable future — rules and regulations being what they are.'

'I hardly see that that's my problem. The children have made enough sacrifices leaving their friends, changing schools . . . '

'I gather from Penny that there was some kind of party tonight and that everyone except you has gone home, leaving you alone with the host. Am I right?'

'Rob, I've merely done the catering for a church do, and now we're working out the costs.'

'Are you, indeed? So you're making some profit from catering?'

'It's nothing to do with you, and I'd rather not continue this conversation. I'll contact you through my lawyer to speed up the divorce proceedings, if that's possible, and suggest you do the same. Then we'll have no need of further contact.'

'Don't be ridiculous. My children are still with you and I'm wondering what sort of example you're setting.'

'How dare you? You conveniently forgot about them when it suited you.'

'Let's not argue, Mads. I'll call you when you're feeling calmer, and can talk some sense.'

'I'm talking sense now and I've no wish to communicate except through my solicitor. Goodbye.'

She switched off, shaking with rage, and turned off the phone, wishing it was a receiver she could slam down.

'Sorry, I should have left you to it, not listened in,' said Guy. 'Hey, come here; you're trembling.'

She took a sip from the glass he handed her. 'I'm so furious with him, but in a way he's right. I'm not behaving very responsibly.'

'You're behaving like a human being, with human needs, and I happen to think you're a warm and wonderful woman the man was crazy to abandon, especially when you've produced four such delightful children with him.'

She gave a small laugh. 'You're good for my ego, do you know that, Guy?'

'Good. Now I'm taking you home. The moment has passed, which is probably just as well.'

'Sorry, I should have stopped . . . '

'Hey, no apologies. Never apologise, never explain. I enjoyed every moment.'

She looked up diffidently and smiled. 'So did I.' She put her glass down on the table. 'Time to go.' She stood up. So did Guy.

'Unfortunately,' he said with a sigh. 'Oh, I nearly forgot. I have a little something for you, partly as thanks for tonight and partly because the twins let slip it was your birthday a few days ago.' He produced a long jewellery box which he proceeded to open. Inside, resting on the blue velvet lining, was a stunning bracelet of small diamonds and sapphires set in white gold.

'Guy, it's beautiful — but it must be priceless. I couldn't possibly accept it.'

'I'd be offended it you didn't. Wrist!'

She obediently held out her wrist while he fastened the beautiful bracelet. 'It's gorgeous. I don't know what to say.'

'You can say thank you, if you like.'

'Thank you, indeed. It's fabulous.' Resting her hands on his shoulders, she stood on tiptoe and kissed his lovely firm mouth.

He took her by the arms and stepped back, smiling down at her. 'Let's get your coat.'

★　★　★

He parked in a dark corner of her drive and leaned over to plant a chaste kiss on her lips. She held back from responding, though her insides were in turmoil, wanting their earlier embraces to reach their logical conclusion.

'Good night, Guy. I'll let you have the receipts for the food sometime.'

'Yes, of course. We'll talk soon.'

10

Maddy let herself in as quietly as she could, thinking everyone would be in bed, but voices in the kitchen informed her otherwise. She went in and was surprised to see Penny sitting at the kitchen table, nursing a glass of brandy and clearly the worse for wear, her face red and blotchy from crying. Hugo lifted his shoulders and made a gesture of helplessness to Maddy. With a quick jerk of her head, she beckoned him into the hall and closed the door to the kitchen.

'What's going on, Hugo?'

'That lady may purport to be your friend but she has a serious chip on her shoulder. Dad phoned while you were out. Apparently Jamie had given him our number. Penny picked up the phone and I couldn't believe what she was saying to him.'

'What do you mean? What was she saying to him?'

'Oh, stuff about your luxurious lifestyle, and the fact that you were, at that very moment, ensconced at the neighbour's with the very attractive — her words not mine — Guy Deverill.'

'Why would she do that?'

'The woman's an absolute bitch.'

'So it would appear. I'd no idea. *In vino veritas*, eh? Anyway, I spoke to your father. He called me on my mobile. I can see now why he was so hostile and unfriendly. Dear Penny's doing, it would seem.'

'She seems to be settled in for the night with the brandy.'

'We'll see about that. You go to bed, love. I'll take care of Penny.'

'Are you sure?'

'Positive.'

She hung up her coat and marched into the kitchen, ready to do battle. The sight of Penny, flushed and tearful, halted her in her tracks.

'Penny, what on earth's the matter?

And what did you say to Rob?'

'I just told him what a nice time you were having with Mr Darcy next door.'

'But why?'

Her tone changed. 'It's amazing the way you always fall on your feet,' she said maliciously. 'In Bournemouth you had the perfect family — four happy, healthy children, shining at school and everything else they touched. You, the perfect mum, producing perfect children, running the perfect home, producing perfect home-cooked meals on cue. The only rotten apple in the barrel was Rob, spreading it around here, there and everywhere.'

'There was only his Canadian colleague . . . '

'You'd like to think!'

Maddy ignored that jibe.

'Penny, why are you being like this?'

'Why do you think? Some of us don't have perfect husbands. We have husbands trying to keep up with the Joneses, children with less-than-straight As, less-than-perfect marriages, and still trying to keep up appearances. But Dawn wasn't so perfect when temptation was put her way, was she? I always thought she was the weakest link, and so it proved.'

'But you didn't know Cassandra was carrying drugs.' Maddy made it a statement. Anything else would be too awful to contemplate. Penny's vicious laugh told her otherwise.

'What kind of a friend are you?'

'How was I to know your perfect little girl was going to have a bad reaction?'

'You're evil, and I've had enough. You're too drunk to leave now but you and Stacey will go first thing in the morning. Go to bed now — unless you'd like me to call your less-than-perfect husband and get him to collect you.'

'I doubt he'd want to get out of his mistress's bed at this hour.'

'So that's what this is about!'

'I'd leave him like a shot but I don't fancy going independent like you.'

'I can believe that. Just go to bed, Penny. There's mineral water in your room.'

'Oh God, you're so-o-o the perfect hostess.'

'I try. Good night.'

Alone, it was Maddy who needed a brandy. Who'd have thought such venom and jealousy had been simmering away in her erstwhile friend? Thinking of Penny's insinuation that she had had a hand in Dawn taking drugs, Maddy went cold. How could anyone do such a thing?

Her thoughts then turned to Guy and those delicious moments they had shared. Perhaps they should know better at their age. On the other hand, life was short. Two clichés that vied with each other. The latter won. She certainly didn't feel guilty. Why should she? As far as she knew, Guy was a free agent. She would soon be free herself. She must contact her solicitor to check that there were no hitches. She'd do that on Monday. That would be tomorrow, she realised, glancing at the kitchen clock. She really must go to bed.

Maddy didn't sleep well. At seven o'clock she decided to get up. The house remained silent as she went downstairs in her dressing gown and made some coffee. Ten minutes later Penny crept into the kitchen.

'I suppose it's pointless to apologise,' she muttered.

'I'm afraid it is, Penny. Anyone who deliberately risks my child's life is no friend of mine.'

'What are you going to do?'

'How do you mean?'

'Well, it would serve me right if you involved the law, but please don't tell Stacey I had anything to do with it.'

'Why not?'

'She would hate me forever, and she would tell her father and he might decide to dump me.'

'God, you're such a fool. I've no intention of telling anyone. Just stay away from my family. How you explain to Stacey is up to you.'

'Explain what?' A bleary-eyed Stacey entered the kitchen.

'I'm afraid we have to go, love,' Penny told her. 'I have things to do.'

'What things?'

'Oh, lots of things.'

'Would you like some breakfast, Stacey?' asked Maddy. 'Croissants and coffee?'

'Did you make the croissants? They look good.'

'I did not, not with the super bakery we have in Dorchester. I'll pop a couple in the Aga, shall I?'

They managed to maintain a normal atmosphere while Stacey ate her breakfast. Penny was the first to push her chair back and stand up. 'Come on, love.'

'But I haven't said goodbye to the twins.'

'Oh, they won't be up for ages,' Maddy told her regretfully. 'I'll say it for you, okay?'

'I suppose, and thank you, Maddy.'

She threw her arms round Maddy and gave her a hug. 'I've had a wonderful time. I wish we lived in the country.'

Penny had the grace to look guilty, Maddy noted as she helped them down with their bags. She breathed a sigh of relief as they drove off, Penny shame-faced, Stacey puzzled.

The young rarely surfaced till lunch-time on a Sunday, and so it was today. When Maddy heard the sound of a lone horse galloping up the field she hoped firstly that it was Guy and secondly that the kids would stay in bed a bit longer. Her hand shook as she filled the kettle and set it to boil.

'Hello there,' came Guy's deep voice. 'May I come in?'

'Of course. No one else is up yet, I'm afraid, and Penny's gone.'

'I thought she was leaving this afternoon.'

'She was, originally, but we've had something of a falling-out.' Maddy explained briefly what had passed between herself and Penny. 'So you see, that is the end of what I considered a beautiful friendship. No one takes risks with my children to satisfy some demented jealousy or whatever. Do sit down.'

'You should report her,' he replied, taking a seat, 'and the niece who supplied the drugs.'

'I don't think we'll be seeing her again, and I don't think she'll do anything like that again either. Am I being a coward?'

'You're being Maddy,' he said, taking her hand and planting a kiss on her palm, which sent pleasurable shock waves through her system.

'I'll pour some coffee,' she said, retrieving her hand and wondering how a woman of her age could experience such fierce sensations.

'Why I called,' he said, accepting the mug she offered, 'was to ask whether you were still interested in having a puppy.'

'We do plan to get one at some point.'

'Not now?'

'Why do you ask?'

'I've just collected two adorable yellow Labrador puppies from my cousin. She does a bit of breeding at her home near Andover, and my dog sired the last litter.'

'*Your* dog? I didn't realise you had one.'

'I don't anymore. Dear Toby, after fulfilling his purpose, so to speak, escaped onto the road. Someone had left the gate open and he was hit by a tractor. As the owner of the sire, I'm entitled, according to best practice, to the pick of the litter. Susie, my cousin, wondered if I'd like a pair. She's so keen on them going to good homes. I told her my neighbour, you, were planning to have one and assured her I thought you would look after one of her precious puppies if you decided to take it. If not, I'll keep them both, so now I'm the owner of two twelve-week-old puppies.'

'Well, we're not exactly geared to

266

housing a dog yet. We'd need to get a bed, feeding bowls, and so on, wouldn't we?'

'Details. Anyway, I don't want to pressure you. That wouldn't be fair. Think about it. Why don't you all come over this afternoon and meet *my* new puppies? There's no church service this Sunday. They're both dogs, by the way, not bitches; very healthy, pedigree as long as your arm. Of course, they'll have to be neutered in a few months' time.'

'Too much information! I'll try and get them all organised to come over after lunch, about three?'

'Perfect. See you then, and thanks for the coffee.' He dropped a kiss on her cheek as he passed, leaving her feeling flushed and girlish, and all the more foolish for feeling so.

They'd reached the pudding stage at lunchtime when Maddy said casually: 'Guy's invited us over to meet his new puppies this afternoon. Anyone want to go?'

'Cool,' said Jamie. 'What kind of puppies?'

'Labradors, he said. Yellow Labradors.'

'Cool,' he said again, a boy of few words. 'Just what I want.'

'Perhaps he'll let you walk them,' said Dawn.

'I'd rather be walking our own.'

They turned up at three on the dot. Dominic, who opened the door to them, was cradling one of the said puppies.

'Oh, isn't he adorable?' Sophie exclaimed, stroking the small creature.

This seemed to necessitate Dominic and Sophie moving closer to each other till their arms were entwined with the puppy and each other.

'Could I hold him?' Dawn asked, edging Sophie aside to take a turn at stroking the puppy and getting close to Dominic.

'Hello, folks. Meet puppy number two,' said Guy, coming up behind Dominic and similarly cradling a puppy.

'Oh, this one's lovely,' said Jamie, gently taking the puppy from Guy.

'Why that one?' asked Hugo. 'They look identical to me.'

'Oh no; they're quite different, just like Dawn and Sophie are different.'

'That's very perspicacious,' said Guy. 'They're identical in colour but actually this one is very slightly lighter in weight, and less rumbustious than his brother. At least he has been today.'

'He's got a lovely face, sort of gentle,' went on Jamie, obviously completely smitten. 'Oh Mum, can we have a puppy just like this one?'

'What do you think, Hugo?'

'I think we'd be a real country family then. I'd love it — but, you know, can we afford it? Vets' bills and things? And who's going to feed it and walk it?'

'I guess I'd be the one to feed it, mostly, and I hope everyone would want to walk it.'

'I will. Oh Mum, can we, please?' begged Jamie.

'What can I say?'

'Say yes, Mum,' said the twins simultaneously.

'I give in.'

'Fantastic!' said Jamie. 'Where can we get one just like this one?' asked Jamie, hugging the puppy close.

Guy exchanged glances with Maddy, raising an eyebrow. She smiled and nodded to him to speak.

'Would you like to have that one, Jamie?'

'*Would I?*'

So it was decided. They would leave it with Guy for a few days while Maddy sorted out bedding and food and contacted the vet about injections. There was also the matter of paying for him.

'Of course, you can visit him any time,' Guy assured them, 'but I think they'd like to be together for a little while now. They still have to get used to being away from their mother. Why don't I bring him over next Saturday?'

'That would be perfect,' Maddy assured him.

'And I'll see you tomorrow to look at the unit.'

'Oh thanks, Guy. I appreciate that.'

'When we get home,' Maddy said as they piled into the car, 'you'd better all check that you've finished your homework.'

'Yes, Mum,' said Dawn. 'And what's that about a unit? What unit?'

'An industrial unit, on the new industrial estate,' Hugo told her. 'Keep up.'

'Wow, it's all happening. So you'll be working away from home, not in a converted outhouse.'

'Well, it's not finally decided,' Maddy told her, increasingly dubious about the idea.

'If you do, who's going to look after Charlie?' Jamie asked.

'Who?'

'The *puppy!*'

'Ah!' Time for some joined-up thinking. 'Maybe the unit isn't such a good idea. It did look like the best option, but of course I hadn't counted on a p . . . Charlie.'

'We can't not have him,' Jamie declared with all the obdurateness of a teenager. 'Please don't say we can't have him.'

'I have to get an income,' Maddy explained. 'What do you suggest I do?'

'I don't know. The flat's almost finished. You can sub-let, can't you?'

'That's a start, I suppose.' The workmen had managed to partition off a corner of the house and turn it into a self-contained flat. 'And I saw an advert looking for accommodation for foreign students. It was very well paid, as far as I can remember.'

They really had no idea of the cost of running a house. Maddy thought fleetingly of the house in Lower Parkstone with the red Aga. Life would have been so simple if they'd bought that. The children would have been near their friends, stayed at the same schools, retained the same interests, and so on. The downside would have been continuing to trust a false friend

272

like Penny, not waking up to this gorgeous view. And never getting to know Guy, a small voice whispered insistently inside her. She had to make this work, however many obstacles Fate and the children put in her path.

'The barns will be ready by next summer,' she said absently. 'If we bought this house instead of renting we could let them out to holiday-makers.'

* * *

On Monday they drove to the industrial estate in Guy's car. The letting agent greeted them enthusiastically, but addressed his remarks to Guy. In the end Guy had to point out his error.

'Actually it's this lady, Maddy, who's interested in taking a unit, if it's suitable. I'm just the chauffeur.'

'I do beg your pardon.' Clearly he didn't altogether believe the explanation, but went on smoothly: 'This way then, Maddy.' He produced the relevant key and let them into one of the brand-new units. 'You'll be number 8,' he said. 'We have a variety of occupants in the other units, including a jewellery-maker, a children's clothes manufacturer, a translation agency, an office equipment provider . . .'

'Quite a variety, as you say. All utilities laid on?'

'Absolutely. As you see, there is a plentiful supply of sockets and every unit has a decent cloakroom. What line are you in, did you say?'

'Catering. I plan to produce ready meals of home-cooked quality.'

'That's quite a market to break into. You'll have to get on to the electricity supplier to install any special wiring you may need for your cooking equipment.'

'Details,' said Guy dismissively. 'Are there any occupants likely to produce noxious smells that might taint the food? Or any producing anything which could prove a fire hazard?'

'No, I can categorically assure you of that. We did have an applicant who wanted to make wrought-iron goods, but we considered that a possible fire hazard, so we turned him down. This is quite a small complex, as you see, and I think the only smells so far could be from your cooking, so hopefully pleasant ones.'

'I think extractor equipment will minimise any problem, in any case' said Guy.

Maddy tried to visualise the space with industrial-sized ovens and mixers, preparation counters and maybe an island in the middle of the room, as well as an office corner with a telephone and computer where orders would be taken and invoices prepared. All she could think of was that it all seemed a bit cold and soulless.

'Seen enough?' asked Guy.

'For now,' she replied. 'I'll have to think about it,' she told the agent.

'Don't take too long. The units are going fast.'

Outside, the agent locked up and shook hands with both of them before they drove away.

'You're very quiet. What do you think?' asked Guy. They'd reached his car, where he opened the passenger door and held it for her to get in.

'I think I wouldn't know where to start. Do you want me to be honest with you, Guy?'

He took his seat and turned to her. 'Honest is good.'

'I'm absolutely terrified. I've never run a business before. It suddenly occurred to me that I know zilch about industrial equipment, suppliers, et cetera. More than that, though — I don't think I want to work in that soulless place. I want to cook in a kitchen where the sun is shining through the window and birds are singing outside. At a more basic level, ready meals are probably not a good way for me to go when you consider the competition already out there.'

He switched on the ignition. 'I see. It may be more difficult to comply with rules and regulations working at home, but I do see what you mean. Is it a definite no, then?'

'Probably. Oh dear, Liz will be furious with me. She already thinks me a lightweight.'

'Fancy a G and T?' he asked, pulling into the gravel forecourt of a delightful-looking country pub.

Having seated her in a corner of the empty bar, he went to fetch the drinks. 'It's quiet in here,' he commented to the landlord.

'It's early yet,' came the reply. 'Trade will pick up at lunchtime.'

'I'm not complaining.'

Even as he spoke, a group of hikers tumbled noisily through the door. 'Let's go through here,' said the first man, leading the way along a corridor to a second bar. 'Morning,' he said in passing to Guy and Maddy. The sound faded to a murmur, the barman went through to the rear counter and they were alone.

'It's not for you, is it, the unit?' asked Guy, turning to Maddy on the small but comfortable bench seat.

'I really don't think it is. I like cooking for people but I like to see the people I'm cooking for. I need to think again.'

Their eyes met and locked, and as thoughts of industrial units and ready meals faded Maddy realised several things. Guy was the most handsome man she had ever met — a man who'd had his share of suffering; a doting, caring father, considerate of those around him. He was also a man who'd been alone for quite a while and who'd built an invisible, defensive screen around himself that kept the world at bay. She herself was a moderately attractive woman living in close proximity, she was attracted to him, and she was in danger of falling in love with him.

Could she let that happen?

Could she stop it happening?

With two fingers he tilted her chin, his head lowered and, as their lips met, the world stood still and she knew it was too late — far, far too late. She was already in love with him, and had been almost from the start.

'I'd better take you home,' he said, drawing away. 'Drink up.'

They barely spoke on the way back. Maddy's thoughts were in turmoil and she wondered if he felt the same. Would he follow her in? Would he want to continue where they'd left off? Would he . . . ?

The car had stopped. She looked round and realised they were in her drive. He turned to her, leaning against his door.

'Maddy,' he said softly, 'what are we going to do?'

'About . . . ?'

'About us. The thing is, I never expected to feel the fire of youth again. It doesn't happen at my age, or so I thought. I never expected to feel as I do about you.' Every word was making her breathless and sending shivers down her spine. 'But I have to remind myself I've reached the age of discretion. I like you, Maddy. I respect you. I'm not in the market for a quick fling, leading nowhere. We each have our family responsibilities. I'm divorced but you're not, as yet, and that could cause complications. We'll have to take things slowly and remain friends for the time being, much as I'd like to take you to bed right now and make love to you.'

She was squirming inside with desire at his words. Her voice came out all shaky. 'I don't know what to say. I'm very attracted to you, Guy.' Madly, hopelessly in love was not what he wanted to hear, she was sure. 'But, as you say, we have to be sensible . . . '

He turned and took her in his arms. 'Could we have a few unsensible moments right now, do you think?'

Her lips parted beneath his, inviting the deepest intimacy. He drew her close, his hand sliding from her shoulder to cup her breast, sending fiery sensations to the core of her being. Were it not for the console dividing the seats, she knew she would have wriggled under him, desperate to feel his weight pressing her down.

'Not exactly a passion wagon,' he muttered, pulling away and getting out of the car.

She was out before he got round to open her door and they walked side by side to the house, his hand in the small of her back. In the cool of her kitchen he took her in his arms and she leaned into his strong frame, feeling soft and ultra-feminine. He traced her curves as if to commit them to memory, running his hands down her back, over her buttocks, pressing her gently into his hardness.

Holding her at the waist he ran his lips along the line of her chin, down the smooth, sensitive skin of her neck, his tongue exploring the hollows at its base. Impatient for more, she lifted her breasts to his exploration. His hands slid upwards, cupping them, his thumbs running gently, tantalisingly across the nubs.

'Oh, please, Guy,' she begged. Was

she begging for more? Was she begging him to stop? He stopped, his hands falling to his sides.

'I'm sorry. I didn't mean to get carried away, when we'd decided to be just friends.'

'You'd better go. I have things to do, decisions to make . . . friend.'

'Sorry. I'm not being much help.'

'You've been a great help, Guy, but now I'd better think of alternatives; and when I've settled on something, I'll make a business plan and get some figures together for my bank manager.'

If she had decided to take the unit, how could she possibly have run the home and looked after the family?

After a call to her solicitor, who assured her everything with regard to the divorce was going to plan and there was nothing they could do to speed things up, she had a quick lunch and then set about trawling the internet to see what kitchen equipment was available. Wherever she worked she'd need rather more than domestic stuff. There seemed to be a lot available relating to the production of cupcakes. She'd love to be doing that — it would be a whole lot more fun than producing ready meals.

Liz phoned and Maddy told her what she had decided about the unit. 'I've been looking through catalogues of kitchen equipment, though, as I do want to do something related to food. It's all alarmingly expensive.'

'Well it's not rocket science, but you'll hardly be receiving industrial-sized orders to start with, so make do with what you have and size up if and when big orders come in.'

'You make it sound so simple. I think I'm doing the right thing turning down the unit, Liz.'

'Okay. Heard anything from my brother?'

'Yes, Rob called the other night while I was at a neighbour's, working out the damage for the church do I catered for. He virtually accused me of having an affair, aided and abetted by my erstwhile friend, Penny, who put the thought in his mind. She was staying with us that night after coming to the church do.'

'Who's the neighbour?'

'His name's Guy Deverill.'

'Really? I know him. He's been at a couple of board meetings when I've been there as the accountant.'

'What was he doing there?'

'Well he trained as a lawyer, but when his second wife left him he became a legal consultant specialising in corporate law, so that he'd be there for his son. He's rather good-looking, and charming too, in a dour kind of way.'

'Yes.' *Not dour with me*, Maddy thought. 'Anyway, when I got home, Penny was off her head, guzzling my brandy and clearly nursing a long-held grudge about my easy life and the way I always fall on my feet. I'd no idea she was jealous of me. The worst thing was her intimating that she was responsible for her niece offering

284

Dawn an 'e' at that disco.'

'Police matter, my dear.'

'She won't do it again. We shan't be seeing them again.'

'I'm glad to hear it. Got to go now. Just remember, I'm here should you need help with a business plan, or if you need financial help . . . '

'You're a gem, Liz. Did I mention Rob thinks they should have a cut of the selling price of the house?'

'He's trying it on. I'm very ashamed of the way my brother's behaved. He had the money from selling out at the agency and left you to finish the mortgage, don't forget.'

'He's finding it hard to get work in Canada.'

'My heart bleeds. Look, I'll come over to see you next week.'

'Great. I'll see you then. Ring first to make sure I'm in.'

'Will do. Bye.'

When Liz had gone Maddy realised she had reached a watershed in her life, poised on the brink of what could be an exciting adventure. She couldn't allow thoughts of Guy or looking after a puppy to cloud her judgment. Neither could she delay, for a new business would require some input of capital and her reserves were dwindling. What was she to do?

11

The children arrived home together at half past four. They filled the kitchen with their cheerful, noisy chatter and swooped on a plate of Welsh griddle cakes Maddy had made to stave off hunger pangs till suppertime.

'What have you been up to today, Mum?' Dawn asked between mouthfuls.

'I've been to look at one of those industrial units,' she replied, dragging her thoughts away from what she and Guy had almost been up to. 'Guy went with me to give a second opinion.'

'Any help?' asked Sophie.

Maddy laughed. 'The sales agent thought Guy was the one interested in the unit so he addressed all his comments to him. He obviously thought I was just the little woman.'

'Guy's little woman,' said Dawn. 'Cool.'

Maddy bent over the sink, concentrating on washing salad vegetables.

'Was the unit any good?' asked Hugo.

'Yes and no. The one I looked at was well-equipped. It had water and electricity and an air-conditioning unit. There was lots of room — too much for what would be quite a small operation, at least to start with. Bottom line, I've decided not to take the unit. Liz probably still thinks I should go for it, but, whatever I decide, she's promised to be there if I need her help.'

'That's good.'

* * *

'When are we going to get Charlie?' Jamie asked a few days later.

'Why don't you talk to Guy about it? Give him a ring.'

'You talk to him.'

Reluctantly Maddy dialled Guy's number. She got Mrs. Frimley.

'He's not here, Maddy,' said Mrs Frimley. 'He got a call from Dominic. Apparently the poor boy's been attacked in Rome — he only flew out yesterday.'

'That's dreadful. What happened?'

'He was mugged by some louts — illegal immigrants or gypsies, according to the Italian police, but apparently that's their standard reaction.'

'Is he badly hurt?'

'I don't know, dearie. He's in hospital, as far as Guy could make out.'

'I'm so sorry. I know this isn't a good time to ask, but the children are really looking forward to having the puppy . . . '

'Oh, well, they're not here at the moment. Guy got his cousin to pick them up and look after them for a bit longer.'

'That's a shame. We could have taken ours. In fact, we could have looked after both of them. Any idea when Guy will be back?'

'He'll be home in a few days. I hope

he brings the boy back with him. Dominic's too young to be going off on his own.'

'I thought he'd gone travelling with friends.'

'They let him down but he was determined to go.'

'He'll be all right, Mrs F.'

'What was all that about, then?' asked Jamie when she'd hung up. 'Aren't we having Charlie, after all?'

'We are soon, love.' She explained what she knew of Dominic's misfortune.

'Is Dominic going to be all right?' asked Sophie.

'I'm sure he will be. I'd better get on with the supper.'

'It's not fair!' Jamie declared. 'Why didn't he leave the puppies with us?'

'I gather it all happened in a bit of a rush. As soon as Guy heard about Dominic, he rang his cousin about the puppies, packed a few things, and was off. Don't worry, love. Guy will be back soon and when he is, we'll take the puppy right away. Okay?'

'S'pose it will have to be.'

* * *

It was Friday and they had just finished eating around the long refectory table in the kitchen. Andy had joined them, as usual, after a lesson with Jamie. They were all feeling replete and relaxed when a tap came on the door and Guy walked in, cradling Charlie in his arms. Jamie's chair scraped back noisily as he hurried from the table to take the puppy. No one but Maddy noticed the way Guy's eyes travelled round the table, settling briefly on Andy and exchanging a hard look, before coming to a halt on Maddy's flushed face. She could see from his expression that he'd got the wrong idea.

'Guy! You're back!'

'Clearly.'

'H-how's Dominic?'

'He's fine, apart from a bit of

bruising and a badly sprained wrist. He didn't want to come home so I drove him in a hired car to some friends in France to recuperate.'

'Do you know Andy?'

The two men eyed each other suspiciously. 'I don't believe we've met.'

'Andy's very kindly helping Jamie with his maths, in exchange for a square meal.'

'I see.'

Andy got up and came forward, offering his hand. 'Andy Carter. I teach at the school this lot attend.'

'Guy Deverill.' Maddy sensed a certain reluctance in his accepting Andy's proffered hand. 'I live next door.'

'I believe I've heard the name.'

None of the children noticed the coolness of the exchange. They had left the table in favour of playing with Charlie.

'I didn't mean to intrude,' said Guy. 'I do need to explain a few things about the puppy, though.'

'He's a nice little fellow,' said Andy, 'but I must away. Homework to mark.'

The chill evaporated along with Andy. Had the others noticed? Maddy wondered.

'Maddy,' Guy began, 'I've made a few notes about feeding, jabs and so on. Where's he going to sleep?'

'I've bought a bed and some bedding for him,' she replied briskly. 'There's that little alcove off the kitchen. I thought he could sleep in there. It's draught-proof and warm.'

'Fine. Give him half a chance and he'll be on your bed.'

'Jamie's, more likely.'

'Not a good idea. These dogs are going to be large. Maddy . . . ' His voice dropped to a soft seductiveness. 'We really need to talk.'

'As they say in the best soaps,' she replied tartly, then sighed. 'Okay, you're right. We need to set a few parameters.' Meaning it wasn't Guy's place to approve her friends or otherwise.

'Mum, come and see Charlie,' Jamie

demanded. 'Look, isn't he just wonderful?'

'He's gorgeous,' she agreed.

'When's Dominic coming back?' Hugo asked.

'When he's well and truly bored with French food and late autumn sunshine,' Guy replied drily.

'No time soon, then.'

'Indeed. Once he's fit he'll either travel on, or come home. Time for Charlie to go outside, I think. Decide the place you want him to use as a loo and he'll probably keep to that spot.'

'A corner of the orchard,' Maddy decided.

All four children piled out.

'Give him some space,' Guy advised, at which they kept their distance but stayed within sight of the puppy, leaving Guy and Maddy alone.

'You want to talk now?' asked Maddy.

'Let's go through,' said Guy, with a backward glance through the window to check that the children were still engrossed in their new pet.

Maddy walked ahead of him to the large sitting room. A fire had been lit and it was very cosy indeed with that and the central heating on. She closed the door and would have taken one of the armchairs beside the fireplace, but Guy caught her arm and pulled her towards him. She looked up, startled, as he held her comfortably against him.

'What is it, Guy?'

'You know what it is. You know how I feel about you.'

'You think you fancy me, Guy. This is a small community with very few available women, and I'm the new kid on the block, so to speak . . . '

'Maddy, don't be absurd. You're a beautiful woman. In my recent travels I've met lots of attractive women, many of them glammed up, coiffed and groomed to the hilt, with all the beauty treatments money can buy. None can hold a candle to you, in your simple jeans and sweatshirts. You have an inner beauty. To me you're the perfect woman. Tonight, when I saw you all casual and domestic, with the family around you and so at ease with Andy, I felt . . . '

'What did you feel?' she asked, tracing one of his dark, arched eyebrows.

'Don't do that,' he begged. 'I felt jealous, that's what I felt. I admit it.'

'What on earth for? Andy's a pleasant enough young man but that's all. It's a business arrangement — Jamie gets tuition, Andy gets a square meal.'

'I know that rationally, but that doesn't stop me feeling jealous.' He took a minuscule step forward and pulled her closer. She felt his needy hardness and echoed his need deep within. He tilted her face with one finger under her pointed chin. The next instant his lips were on hers and the flame of desire leapt between them. She wriggled against him, fitting her curves to his steely frame. After a while, some remaining vestige of common sense made her extricate herself, though with some difficulty.

'We mustn't, Guy.'

'I know we mustn't. I also know we both want to. The trouble is the total impossibility of a decent relationship.'

There and then she would have settled for an indecent one.

'What do you mean?'

'I don't want a hole-in-the-corner affair, but the barriers are huge. I have a son, you have four children. All their feelings need to be considered.'

'They all like you — and Dominic, and that's a start.'

'And I like them, too, of course, but they've just been abandoned by their father. There will be some raw feelings beneath the surface, particularly with Jamie, I believe.'

'Yes, I think you're right. We'll just have to settle for being friends and neighbours for now.'

'God, how boring. I'll probably go out of my mind wanting you every time I see you.'

'Will you, indeed.' She smiled coquettishly and, acting quite uncharacteristically, she trailed her fingers from his shoulder, down his chest and across to his thigh, just skimming the bulge of his arousal. 'If it's any consolation, you won't be suffering alone.'

'Good,' he replied, grabbing the wandering hand and lifting it to kiss her palm softly and at length.

There were sounds of voices as the children burst into the house, presumably with the puppy, Charlie. They joined them in the kitchen.

'He did it,' Jamie informed them. 'Pees and poos everywhere.'

'Which you can clean up in daylight.'

'Oh, must I?'

'Of course. We don't want the place to stink like a doggie loo.'

'Okay. Here, Charlie.' But Charlie had curled up on the rug near the Aga and fallen instantly asleep.

'Oh, before I go, Maddy, there's a place in Dorchester I'd like you to see, which may be a happy alternative to the industrial unit or working at home.'

'Tell me more.'

'I'd rather show you. Could you spare a couple of hours tomorrow morning?'

'Very mysterious.'

'Can I come?' asked Hugo.

'Why not?'

'Can we come?' asked Dawn.

'Let's all go,' said Guy.

'I'd rather stay here with Charlie,' said Jamie. 'I don't feel too good.'

'Really?' Maddy felt his brow. 'You're not feverish, but it would be nice for Charlie if you stayed with him.'

'I'll pick you up at ten then, all right?'

★ ★ ★

'Where are we going?' Maddy asked.

Guy had parked his Land Rover and they entered a twisting alleyway not unlike the one where they'd first met. 'You'll see. Oh, by the way, they caught the villains who mugged me. They're now under lock and key in the young offenders' institution on Portland, where hopefully they'll be sorted out.'

299

'Good. Who were they?'

'A couple of teenagers with no jobs, no money, probably no hope, and bored out of their skulls.'

'Hardly an excuse.'

'I know, but it's an explanation of sorts.' They turned a corner. 'Here we are.'

The little road widened. Set back from the road was a small terrace of shops, among them an ironmonger's with an unusual variety of goods, a hairdresser's, a bookshop and a fourth shop which was empty.

'This is it,' said Guy, producing a key and opening the door. 'In you go.' And in they all went. He closed the door. 'What do you think of this, Maddy? First impression?'

'Well, it's certainly different from that cold and impersonal industrial unit. It's really sweet. I like the double bay windows and those swirly glass centres. Bull's eyes, I think they're called.'

'I believe so. They resulted at the end of the glass-making process and used to be thrown away. It then became fashionable to use them to give a window character, so they weren't wasted. You don't get them with modern glass-making processes.'

'That's cool,' said Dawn, impressed.

'This could be your shop, Maddy. You didn't like the industrial unit, did you?'

'To be really honest, I hated it.'

'Well this has more character, but could you cook here? At present there's a kitchen at the rear end and living accommodation on the two upper floors. How do you think you would you use it? Showrooms? Store-rooms? A tea-room, maybe? What do you think?'

'I like it a lot. I can imagine working here. It's got atmosphere. I could almost say it's got soul. How about a cake shop cum tea-room?'

'It's too big for a cake shop,' said Sophie.

'Of course it is, and I don't intend to live above the shop, either, so I could use all the space for — what? I'd like to have a café, where everything would be homemade and as wholesome as possible, apart from some yummy cakes. And what should I call it? It could be Cupcakes and . . . and what?'

'Candlesticks?' Guy supplied.

'I like that.'

'So do I,' said Dawn.

'And that's what I shall sell, among other things. Candlesticks, beautiful lamps and lampshades. Gorgeous accessories . . . '

'Artisan jewellery and pashminas . . . ' said Dawn.

'And mirrors . . . ' added Sophie.

'Mirrors are an excellent idea,' said Maddy. 'It's a bit dark in here. Mirrors would reflect the light.'

'I meant to sell.'

'I know you did, but they could also brighten the place up. It gets better and better. Let's explore the rest.'

'You could paint the walls light colours,' suggested Guy.

'I could, but actually I like antique reds and greens. Imagine the walls in rich colours with gold-framed paintings and mirrors, for sale as well as display of course, and spotlights . . . '

'No shortage of ideas.'

'I'd want to sell beautiful things, as Dawn has suggested. Upmarket things. I think in a historic county town like Dorchester items such as artisan jewellery and pottery would go down a treat. There are quite a few craftsmen and women in the area, I've discovered. I'm sure some of them would welcome a ready outlet for their creations. We'd have to have candlesticks, of course, to justify the name. We could drape scarves and jewellery over them. Oh, you are clever, Guy.'

He smiled indulgently. 'You're getting carried away, Maddy. An Aladdin's cave of beautiful things — have you forgotten the cupcakes bit, though?'

'Not at all. I'd want to keep the little kitchen at the rear of the shop for the staff. It's too small for anything else. I envisage the ground floor for smaller items such as handmade cards, small toys and games for children, for instance. Upstairs there would be a showroom displaying pricier stuff, and at the back a café selling tea, coffee, savoury snacks and of course cupcakes.'

'Where did all that come from?'

'I just feel inspired, looking at the place.'

'And customers would have to go through the shop, up the stairs and through the first-floor showroom, where hopefully they'd be seduced by the wonderful things on offer.'

'Hopefully. Thank you, Guy, for finding this place.'

'It's only just come on the market. If you want it, now's the time to decide.'

'What about licences and things like that?'

'Details,' he said, and she smiled. He really was a lovely man, and a reassuring one.

'Mum, can Sophie and I work here at weekends?'

'That's a brilliant offer. Of course you can.'

'What's the pay like?' asked Dawn.

Maddy laughed. 'Don't worry, you'll be paid.'

* * *

So with all the family on board — including Jamie, who was convinced by his siblings' enthusiasm — it was decided.

He was trying to ignore a sore throat and raised temperature, not wishing to put a damper on things and not wanting to miss the next football match, but Maddy sensed he was more than a little off-colour and called the doctor anyway. She guessed it was worse than he admitted. Fortunately a course of antibiotics soon sorted him out.

* * *

A bit of publicity brought in a bewildering array of offers for shop-fittings and goods and services to help start up the business. Maddy was not so ignorant as to believe everything that was claimed, but she realised there would be some gold among the dross. She spent an evening going through the offers which were spread out on the dining-room table, picking out the ones that looked worthy of further consideration.

'How's it going?' asked Hugo, wandering in and placing a cup of coffee at her elbow.

'My saviour,' she said. 'Thanks, love. Finished your homework?'

'All I intend to do this evening,' he assured her, rubbing tired eyes. 'I have a couple of free periods tomorrow to catch up.'

'Good. I've sorted everything into piles: rejects, possibles and hopefuls.'

'Can I take a look?'

'I'd be glad if you would,' she replied, sipping the welcome brew. 'This is delicious. By the way, I got the divorce papers through to sign.'

'And have you? Signed them, I mean?'

'I have. There's no point in hanging fire, is there, especially as your father's agreed to a clean break. I expect he will sign his quite promptly. I mean, with me pushing and her pulling, what possible reason would he have not to?'

'Yes. It's a shame, though, isn't it?'

'In what way?'

'In the way that we once enjoyed a great family life with plenty of fun, no money worries . . . '

'You think I should take him back, if that were possible?'

'No, far from it. I'm enjoying our new life. The old one was a sham. Holly wasn't the first, it's beginning to emerge.'

'Which I, being the wife, was the last to know, but actually the first to suspect.'

'You're worth better than that. I'm not saying I never want to see Dad again. After all, he's our father. But I think this will work out just fine.'

Leaving Maddy to wonder what Hugo's 'this' included.

* * *

It was early November and autumn was beginning to bite. In the past, Maddy would have already been planning for Christmas. This year Christmas plans would have to wait as the new business took precedence. She was so busy going back and forth to the shop, visiting suppliers and marketing to potential clients, that she didn't notice how poorly Jamie had begun to look.

'Are you okay, half-pint?' Hugo asked him at breakfast one morning.

'Yeah. I think I've got another cold coming on, though.'

Maddy, alerted to his plight, felt his forehead. 'You've got a temperature, love. I think you'd better have a day in bed. You had that sore throat only a couple of weeks ago, too.'

'I hope it's not chicken pox. Three of the kids in my class are absent with it.'

'Oh, gross,' said Dawn. 'We're not going to get spotty, are we?'

'You're not,' Maddy assured her. 'You

others had it together before Jamie was born.'

'That's a relief.'

'Dawn, you're so heartless,' said Sophie, uncharacteristically critical of her twin. 'You look terrible, Jamie. Poor lamb.'

'Thanks,' he replied drily. 'Can I have a paracetamol, Mum? I've got a stinking headache.'

'Sure.' She popped a tablet in a glass of water. 'You take that. I'll make up your bed and fill a hot-water bottle.'

The others went off to catch the school bus. Maddy revised her schedule for the day. Suddenly she was glad she had decided against the unit, but was now a bit worried about the plans for the shop. She was sure it was right for her and she wanted to make it work, but she couldn't leave Jamie alone when he was ill. At mid-morning, Guy phoned.

'Hi, Maddy. I wondered if you'd all like to come over this evening for supper? Dom's back, and I think we should talk to the children; try out the waters, so to speak. Apart from that, I just want to see you.'

'I want to see you, too, Guy, but we can't come, I'm afraid. Jamie's not well. I've just packed him off to bed with a temperature and a bad headache. He's going nowhere this evening, and I can't leave him when he's ill.'

'Poor kid. I'm sorry to hear that. Anything I can do?'

'I'm just going to stick around here today and make some phone calls. You could come and eat with us this evening, if you like — you and Dominic. We haven't seen him since he went away. As to testing the waters, let's leave that for another time, okay?'

'Of course. Children come first. Sevenish?'

'Yes, we'll eat at half past.'

'I look forward to it.'

In the afternoon Maddy, having spent the rest of the day making phone calls and doing sums, prepared a straightforward meal of roast lamb and vegetables and apple pie. No time for fancy touches, but she would make sure the accompaniments were perfect: mint sauce using fresh mint from the garden, homemade redcurrant jelly, and beautiful light pastry for the pie.

She had just come down from taking Jamie a jug of lemon barley water when the phone rang. To her surprise it was Val, her Bournemouth cleaner.

'This is a nice surprise, Val. How are you?'

'We're both fine, but we're rather bored. We've been thinking and we've decided we'd like to follow your example and move out to the country. If we were close enough, maybe I could work for you again.'

'That would be marvellous, Val. I'm in the throes of setting up a business, so I need all the help I can get. I'm about to open a shop in Dorchester. I'll need a cleaner there as well as here.'

'We're going to start going round the Dorchester estate agents right away. Can you recommend any, Maddy?'

'Well, not really. As you know I bought this house through Simon.

Look, I can't talk long now. I'm just cooking supper and I've got Jamie ill in bed upstairs.'

'What's wrong with him?'

'I'm not sure. I thought it was a feverish cold but he looks really poorly. First he's too hot, then he's shivering.'

'Have you called the doctor?'

'No, not yet. I don't want to call him out for nothing more than a cold.'

'Call him, Maddy. I can tell you're concerned.'

Maddy went back upstairs again. 'Do you feel any better, Jamie?'

'Worse. I've got a rash on my legs. Do you think it's chicken pox?'

'Let's see.' She looked at the purply-red striations on his legs with concern. They were nothing like the chicken-pox rash she remembered.

'I'm calling the doctor, love.'

'I need to go to the bathroom, but my feet hurt. So do my hands.'

'I'll help you.'

Easier said than done. He was bigger than her now but she helped him hobble there and back again, then called the doctor.

'I'm coming right away,' he said after she'd explained the symptoms.

He was there in minutes. She was quite sure it would have been days in Bournemouth. 'Ye-es,' he murmured after looking at the rash and taking Jamie's pulse and temperature. 'Well it's not chicken pox, but it could be a reaction to the virus he had recently. I'm pretty sure it's something called Henoch-Schoenlein purpura. It generally follows a bout of pharyngitis, which is probably what that sore throat was.'

'So how do we treat it?' Maddy asked lightly, hiding the terror she felt inside.

'Rest and plenty to drink. You're doing the right thing. I'll call again tomorrow, Jamie. Shall we?' He gestured to Maddy with his head and she led the way downstairs.

'Is that all we can do?'

'We could treat it with steroids, but they may not help and they do have side effects. I'll just say this — if you notice any unusual bleeding, call an ambulance and get him to hospital right away.'

Maddy was trying not to shake, really frightened now. 'He is going to be all right, isn't he?'

'I'm sure he is, but he's very poorly at the moment. You don't live with his father, do you?'

'No. He left us and went to live in Canada.'

'I see. Well, it may be a good idea to call him. I imagine he would want to know when his son's so ill.'

'I'll do that.'

Which she did, once the doctor had left. 'Rob, look, I'm sorry to bother you and I don't want to worry you, but Jamie is really not very well. I think he'd like to see you.'

'That boy's such a baby. I can't just take off like that. Flights cost money and it's in rather short supply at the moment.'

'Right.'

'Okay. What's wrong with him?'

'He's got a post-viral infection, something to do with his blood. The doctor suggested I call you.'

'He'll be fine. He's a strong boy. At the moment I'm trying to set up a business.'

'You and me, too.'

'Come off it. You're sitting pretty. I've been working my nuts off in Holly's brother's logging business. It's damn hard work but I've got to do something.'

'You're not coming, then?'

'I'm not. I can't. Keep in touch. I'll be getting that Skype thing Hugo suggested soon.'

When she had put the receiver down, Maddy was shaking not with terror but with rage. She didn't care that Rob had abandoned her, but how dare he write off his children!

Apprised of the situation, Hugo, when he arrived home, offered to carry his brother downstairs. 'It's depressing being all alone when you're ill. I remember it well.'

'You can ask him if he wants to come downstairs, love.'

Hugo was soon back. 'He doesn't want to be moved and he says he doesn't want any supper. I'll take him up some more water soon. He's still got half a jug.'

'Shall I ask Guy and Dominic not to come?'

'No. It'll be good for you. Guy seems to give off a kind of strength, and you could do with some of that.'

★   ★   ★

They were finishing off the apple pie when they heard Jamie calling weakly from upstairs. Maddy was up like a shot, Guy close behind.

'My nose is bleeding,' Jamie sobbed, 'and so's my bottom.'

Maddy looked at Guy, panic-stricken. 'I must call an ambulance.'

'No need. I'll take him. Lucky we came in the car.' He wrapped Jamie in a blanket while Maddy put together a few toiletries and clothes for him. As an afterthought she added a change of clothes for herself. They went off with a few brief explanations, leaving the others totally bewildered. As they drove towards Dorchester, some instinct made Maddy decide to call Val.

'What is it, Maddy? How's Jamie?'

'We're taking him to hospital — that is, a neighbour and I are. Thing is, can I ask you a favour, Val?'

'Anything.'

'I wondered if you could come and stay for a couple of days. I need to be with Jamie. I'm not leaving him alone in hospital, and well . . . I thought you might like to use my place as a base while you look at properties.'

'Of course we'll come. We'll be there within the hour.'

'Oh, bless you. I'll warn Hugo to organise the guest room.'

'Don't worry about a thing. I can make up the bed and clear the supper things — unless the girls have suddenly become domesticated.'

Maddy smiled. 'They can be when it suits them. Thanks, Val.' She switched off. 'And thank you, Guy. You seem to be always ferrying my children to or from hospital.' Jamie, still wrapped in the blanket and held by Guy, seemed to be asleep. 'Is he all right?'

'Well he's still breathing, if that's what you mean, but I'll be glad to get him to a doctor.'

He parked in an ambulance bay. At sight of the tall man with his human bundle, a bevy of doctors and nurses surrounded them and, apprised of his symptoms, directed them to an empty cubicle where a senior doctor was summoned.

'Yes, your G.P. is almost certainly right. We'll keep him in a side ward overnight and run some tests. Do you want to stay with him?'

'Mum?' Jamie whispered.

'Of course. I'll be here, Jamie.'

Guy stood by, looking and probably feeling helpless. 'Do you want me to stay, Maddy?'

'I'd like you here but there honestly isn't much point. I'd like a coffee and a bottle of water, though, before you go.'

'Your word is my command. I think I spotted a coffee machine in the corridor.'

He soon returned with coffee and a bottle of water; then, leaving Jamie with the medical staff, Maddy walked with Guy to the main door. There he cupped her face in his hands, looking down into her frightened, caring eyes.

'I love you, Maddy. I want you to know that. I don't want to intrude but if you need a friend, I'm here for you.'

'Thank you, Guy. Thank you for being there and thank you for giving me space. I'll call you tomorrow. Tell the kids Jamie's going to be fine.'

'I'm sure he is. It sounds trite but do try not to worry. Jamie's in the best place.'

With which she went back inside to spend a sleepless night on an uncomfortable mattress on the floor of Jamie's side room.

12

Maddy stayed at the hospital for several days and nights, trying to keep Jamie's spirits up. At the same time she was mulling over all the things she should be doing. Apart from keeping the house running, which Val would hopefully manage to do in her absence, there was her new project, Cupcakes and Candlesticks, hanging fire. The flat was finished and ready to let, and she would need to vet the new occupant herself. Then, last but not least, there was Guy Deverill, and their declared love for each other.

The twins were at an age when they needed subtle supervision. What if Dawn went off the rails again and did something stupid?

On the third day, Dawn and Sophie paid a surprise visit. 'Hi, Mom,' said Sophie 'How's the brat?' she asked lovingly. 'Jamie, what're you doing malingering here?'

Jamie turned towards her, lying on his side, and managed a wan smile. His face was striped with purple, as were his arms, resting over the sheet.

'Jamie, baby,' said Dawn. 'What've you been doing? You're covered in bruises!'

'I'm all right,' he mumbled. 'I just want to go home.'

'I don't think they'll let you just yet,' said Dawn. 'Come here. Give me a hug.'

'Gently,' Maddy warned.

'Sorry, don't want to hurt you, little one.'

Funny how they came out with all these baby names when Jamie was ill. He was taller than the twins now, but still the youngest and at the moment so very vulnerable.

'You are going to be all right?' Sophie asked. 'He is going to be all right, isn't he, Mum?'

'Of course he is.'

Nevertheless a dart of fear pierced her heart. What if? What if? This was when a supportive husband equally concerned for their child would have been so wonderful.

A nurse approached the bed and produced a thermometer.

'Can we bring you anything, Jamie? Books, CDs, anything?' asked Sophie.

'No,' he replied, unable to move with a thermometer in his ear. 'Just want to go home.'

'That won't be for a while, Jamie,' the nurse informed him cheerfully. 'He's not drinking enough, or eating properly, and he tries to refuse his medicine.'

'My mouth's sore.'

'I'll get something for it.'

Jamie put his tongue out at the nurse's retreating back.

'Oh, nearly forgot,' said Sophie. 'We've brought you some photographs.' She retrieved an envelope from her bag and proceeded to show Jamie the half-dozen pictures she'd taken of Charlie. To their dismay, a fat tear rolled down his cheek as he looked at them.

'Could they bring Charlie in, Mum, please?'

'I'm pretty certain they don't allow dogs in hospital, darling, but I'll ask.'

'Oh, I nearly forgot,' said Dawn. 'Robin's having a bonfire party at the vicarage for Guy Fawkes, but he's going to delay it till you're back home, Jamie.'

'Great — it gives me a headache just thinking about it right now. Sorry, it's very good of him. Thank him for me, okay?'

'Of course.'

'Has Dad phoned?'

'Not yet. I'm sure he will soon, though.'

So uncaring. So unlike Guy. Maddy thought of Guy's late visit the previous evening. Jamie had been asleep so she'd gone out into the corridor with him.

'Here. Mrs F's sent a cool-bag full of goodies. There's pâté and cheese, and some figs, dates and mandarin oranges — a taste of the coming festivities.

They're for both of you, as a change from hospital food.'

'Oh God, it'll soon be Christmas. I can't be in here till then. I've got several orders for cakes and enquiries about parties.'

'You're not to worry about a thing outside this hospital. We've got a good team, with Val and Reg looking after the house, cleaning and cooking and making fires, between searching for a property of their own. The boys, Dom and Hugo, have helped chop a pile of cordwood into logs, too.'

'Which came from where?'

'My little log man. He's very good. Think of it as an early Christmas present.'

'You're so kind, Guy.'

'Nonsense. There is so little I can do. Only the doctors can help Jamie, but what about that ex-husband of yours? Does he know his son's ill? Is he coming over?'

'I phoned him at the beginning, and again since Jamie was admitted here,

I've left a message on his mobile.'

Guy shook his head in disgust. 'Let's get some coffee.'

'I don't want to go far from the ward.'

'It's only round the corner and there are nurses on duty.'

He let them know where they were going, though, for Maddy's peace of mind. They walked back from the coffee machine, sipping the hot brew and agreeing that it was indeed hot and wet but that was all that could be said for it.

★   ★   ★

That evening, after the twins' visit, Maddy felt her mobile vibrating in her pocket and immediately felt guilty. The use of mobiles was discouraged, though some people insisted they didn't interfere with hospital equipment. Patientline was beyond the reach of many patients, who were often suffering from a sudden lack of income and the added cost of travelling to the hospital. By comparison Maddy was lucky. She hurried onto the balcony.

'Hello?'

'Mum?' It was Hugo. 'Can you get Jamie over to the window overlooking the garden?'

'I don't know. He's very weak. I can try, though.'

'I promise you it'll be worth it.'

She went back inside. 'Jamie? Are you up to getting over to the window over there?'

'Why?' he asked sullenly.

'It's Hugo's idea — a surprise.'

'Okay.'

Maddy helped him out of bed, hiding her dismay at the bruises on his legs where his pyjamas had ridden up and on his stomach where his pyjama jacket gaped. Slowly, with Maddy's support, he hobbled to the window.

'Oh look, Mum.' He was laughing and crying at the same time for there in the garden below was Charlie, his beloved Labrador puppy, on a long lead held by Hugo, fat and floppy and altogether adorable, bouncing around and trying to escape his leash. Behind Hugo stood Dom, who must have chauffeured them to the hospital.

'He's grown, hasn't he, Mum? Oh, I wish I could touch him.'

'Soon, sweetheart. I think he's grown in the few days since I saw him.'

'What are you up to, out of bed, Jamie?' demanded a staff nurse. She moved forward to see. 'Oh, what a sweetie! Is he yours?'

'Yes,' Jamie replied, choked by weakness and emotion.

'Well then, the sooner you're home, the sooner you can play with him. Keep drinking and stop fussing about the medicine and food.'

'Yes, staff.'

As they watched, Hugo handed the lead to Dominic and disappeared inside the building. Soon he was walking into the ward, giving Jamie a bear hug.

'Ouch!'

'Careful, Hugo; he bruises easily.'

'Sorry. How are you, squirt?'

'How do I look?' Jamie shuffled back to bed.

'Pretty terrible, but I'm told it's not terminal. Mum, do you want to go back with Dom for a couple of hours while I stay with Jamie?'

'Don't go, Mum.'

Maddy thought about it. 'I don't think it's a good idea, Hugo, but thanks for the offer. Once I get home, I'll get involved in everything and won't be able to leave. I'll stay here a few more days, but then I must go home for a few hours each day. There's so much to sort out.'

'I'll go and let Dom know. I can make my own way home later. Oh, a surprise visitor.'

Maddy looked up to see Andy Carter walk in, accompanied by a nurse. She felt a pang of disappointment and knew she had wanted it to be Guy.

'Hi, Andy.'

'I don't want to intrude,' Andy began.

'You're not intruding. Nice of you to

drop in but, as you see, he's in no state for a lesson.'

'I realise that, but I'm missing the nosh,' he told Maddy with a grin. 'You're going through the mill a bit, aren't you, Jamie?'

'You could say that.'

'There's a bit of self-interest in my visit. I have a publisher interested in my book after reading a partial, and . . . '

'That's wonderful, Andy.'

'Thanks. Anyway, although it's finished in draft form, I need to polish it up and for that I need a bit of peace and quiet. The family living above me are getting noisier by the day. I think the baby's teething or something, and the toddler's racketing around on some wheeled vehicle or other . . . I'll get to the point.'

'Please do.'

'I'd like to rent the flat, Maddy.'

'Okay. I don't see why not. It's certainly ready. I'll talk to Guy.'

'Oh. Can't we do it between ourselves?'

'We could, but . . . '

'Thing is, the publisher wants the book in two weeks. Perhaps I could move in temporarily?'

'I'm sorry, I really can't think about it now, Andy.'

Which was when Guy walked in, accompanied by Robin Groves, their vicar. A nurse bustled in after them. 'I'm sorry. We've relaxed the rules up to now with visitor numbers but Jamie needs peace and quiet. Could you go in two at a time, please?'

'I'd better go,' said Andy. 'But think about it, Maddy.'

'I will.'

Robin went out with Andy, leaving Guy and Hugo. 'What did he want?' Guy asked, clearly irritated.

'He wants to rent the flat.'

'I see. And what do you want, Maddy?'

'I need a reliable tenant. He needs somewhere quiet to work on his book.'

'So?'

'I'd like a proper agreement drawn

330

up, while Andy wants a more casual arrangement.'

'Do you want me to have an agreement drawn up?'

'Well, it would be useful, but I can't let you. You've done so much already.'

'It's fine. Hugo can help.'

'Could I? Don't you need a solicitor?'

'You get a form from a stationer and fill in the details. It's quite straightforward and I'll look over it, of course.'

'I was forgetting you're a lawyer.'

'Get two copies in case you make a mistake.'

'Will do.'

'Is that all right then, Hugo?'

'Sure. Right now I'm wondering if I can cadge a lift back.'

'I'll just grab a coffee while Robin comes in, then you could go back with him.'

'Okay.' Hugo looked puzzled. 'I thought I could go back with you.'

'Well, you could, but I've only just arrived. I'll tell Robin he can come in now. He probably won't stay long.'

Robin strolled in alone. 'It seems I've got myself a temporary lodger,' he told them. 'Andy, the chap who just walked out. He still wants to rent your flat but he's desperate for some peace and quiet right now.'

'Oh dear. People do get sucked into our problems. It's as though someone has thrown a pebble into a pond and the ripples are spreading wider and wider.'

'Am I the pebble?' Jamie asked.

'Only in a nice way, love. I'm actually astonished and delighted the way people have rallied round.'

'So you've taken pity on Andy, then?' Guy asked Robin.

'He seems a nice enough chap, and it'll give you time to sort out an agreement, Maddy, if you decide to let the flat to him.'

'That's really kind of you, Robin.'

'So, how's our invalid today?' He walked round and sat on a chair beside the bed. 'Are you feeling any better, Jamie?'

'Not really.'

'Some of these viruses take time.'

'Some of these viruses are odd. This one is, anyway, apparently. A whole gaggle of doctors were in here this morning from different hospitals, standing round the bed staring and asking daft questions.'

'You've become a celebrity! Anyway, I'm not staying but if you fancy a game of chess, let me know through your mum. Meanwhile, we'll be praying for you in church.'

'If you must.'

'Do you want a lift home, Hugo?'

'Yes, please. See you soon, Jamie. Be good and get better quickly. Charlie's missing you.'

'Has Dad called?'

Maddy winced inwardly and Hugo hesitated. 'Not yet. We haven't managed to speak to him but we've left messages. At least he's on Skype now. I'll try calling him again tonight.'

'Bye, Maddy,' said Robin. 'Take care of yourself.'

'You, too.'

* ★ *

'I've brought you a few goodies, Jamie,' said Guy, gently depositing a large bag on the bed tray.

'Thanks, Guy.' Jamie withdrew the contents: several brand new novels, a book of Sudoku and a Rubik's cube in a bubble pack. 'Oh, cool, some of my favourite authors — and I've always wanted a Rubik's cube. That's really kind of you.' Having examined the contents of the bag, Jamie let them fall to the coverlet and sank back onto the pillows, exhausted. 'I'm so fed up feeling like this,' he said weakly.

Maddy took his hand. 'You'll be fine soon. You've had a bit of activity and excitement today. That's why you're tired.'

'I have, haven't I?'

'Some of your mates have phoned. They'd like to visit but I suggested they leave it a week or so.'

'How long am I going to be in here?'

'Depends how quickly you recover.'

'It might be a good thing to see some of his pals,' put in Guy. 'Cheer you up, Jamie. Anyway, it's up to you. Say the word and your mum will let them know they can visit. I doubt they'd allow a whole football team in at once, though.'

* * *

Maddy called Andy at the vicarage that evening.

'Hi, Maddy. This is unexpected. How's the invalid?'

'Still poorly, but I'm beginning to detect a slight improvement. Hugo brought Charlie, the puppy, over today and he was able to see him through the window. It's given him a bit of an impetus to get better.'

'That sounds positive.'

'The reason I'm calling is firstly to say I'm glad you've sorted out somewhere to live for now.'

'Yes, Robin's been very accommodating.'

'Literally. Secondly, we think it would

be a good idea for some of Jamie's school friends to visit, if they'd like to.'

'I'm sure they'd love to. He's very popular at school.'

'I can believe that from the piles of cards he's received.'

'I'll spread the word, and I look forward to moving into the flat when I've finished editing.'

'How's the book going?'

'Fine. I'm almost ready to send it off for copy-editing.'

'That's good. I think we'll be resuming the tuition for Jamie after Christmas.'

'Great. I've been thinking — he may well appreciate some notes from his other teachers to study and catch up a bit. Shall I arrange that?'

'That would be marvellous. See you soon, then.'

* * *

On Sunday morning Jamie sat up in bed and announced: 'Do you know,

Mum — I feel a lot better. It's as if I've been full of a poison and now it's slowly seeping away.'

'Well that's fantastic, Jamie.'

'You can go home today if you like, Mum, but I'd quite like you to come back this evening.'

'Well of course I will. Are you sure you'll be all right today?'

'I'm sure.'

★ ★ ★

Maddy thought she'd surprise everyone so she didn't warn them of her return. In the event it was she who got the surprise.

She took a taxi home and walked round to the back door. Hearing the sounds of digging and some classical music playing quietly, she walked along the path and down the steps to the vegetable patch. There she found Andy working away.

'What on earth are you doing, Andy?'

'Maddy!' He switched off his radio.

337

'We didn't expect you back yet.' We? 'I thought I'd double-dig this patch ready for sowing. Oh, is that all right?'

'But I didn't ask you to.'

'Well, after I'd sent off my manuscript, I was lost for something to do in my spare time. I believe I told you my family run a market garden in Worcestershire. It's one of my passions. I drew up a draft plan . . . Oh dear, I've rather overstepped the mark, haven't I?'

'I don't know what to say. I haven't budgeted for a gardener . . . '

'Oh, I don't want payment. I just enjoy doing it — working in this lovely environment, listening to my favourite music. Oh God, I'm sorry.'

'Please don't be. It's really kind of you and I can see you're making a professional job of it.'

'So I can carry on?'

She smiled. 'You can carry on.'

Inside, she got a more unpleasant shock.

The kitchen was a shambles. Last night's dinner dishes were piled in the sink and on the draining boards. The table held the detritus of what looked like breakfast for two.

Maddy wandered through the house in search of someone to explain what was going on. The downstairs rooms were empty and in need of a clean. Enraged and disappointed by what seemed like total neglect of their home, Maddy walked into the hall and banged the dinner gong.

There were sounds of movement upstairs and the next moment Sophie appeared on the landing in her nightdress, followed by Dawn, similarly attired.

'What's going on?' asked Sophie. Then, with obvious delight, 'Mum! You're home!' She whizzed down the stairs at breakneck speed, closely followed by her twin. The next instant they shared a three-people hug. Maddy felt the tears, long held back, begin to flow.

'Hey, you're home now. Sit down and we'll make some coffee.'

'If you can find a cup, or even the coffee machine,' she replied tersely.

'What do you mean?' asked Dawn.

They all went into the kitchen, where it was the twins' turn to be surprised. 'Oh God, look at the mess! That bloody Val! She said she'd clean up after they'd eaten last night. We went out for a pizza with Hugo and Dom. They've even left their breakfast things. Oh, I'm so sorry, Mum.'

'But where are they, Val and Reg?'

'House-hunting, I expect,' Dawn replied. 'Really, Mum, they do take liberties. They've been living here rent-free, helping themselves to food . . . '

'And drink,' added Sophie. 'And they've hardly done a hand's turn around the place.'

'I never realised. Val sounded so keen to help.'

'Herself,' muttered Dawn.

Even as she was talking, Maddy was automatically clearing up and stacking the dishwasher. How dare they treat her beautiful home like this!

'There, that didn't take long,' said Sophie, wiping down the table while Dawn organised the coffee.

'Where's Hugo? He's usually up by now.'

'Ah! Well after we got home, Dawn and I went straight to bed. Hugo was going to have a drink with Dom. Haven't seen him since.'

Maddy set off upstairs. Hugo didn't drink — well, hardly at all. She knocked on his door and, getting no reply, went in. He was lying on his back, still half-dressed, softly snoring.

'Hugo!'

'Uh?' He sat up quickly and then put his hand to his head, peering at her through bloodshot eyes. 'God, I feel awful. Mum, you're home!'

'And not before time! Hugo, what's been going on?'

'Sorry, Mum. We had to go out to get away from them.'

'Them? Who? Do you mean Val and Reg?'

'I do mean Val and Reg. We couldn't

stand any more of their microwaved ready meals and the constant blare of soaps on the television. They even had the cheek to complain about the noise of music practice. Oh Mum, Val may be well-meaning, but Reg is a complete slob and she seems to be right under his thumb.'

'I see. Well, they'll have to go. I'll be home properly soon . . . '

'And meanwhile we can manage — honestly, Mum. It's the holidays soon, anyway.'

'I'll send one of the twins up with paracetamol.'

'It's okay. I'm coming down.'

It was a delight to reclaim her kitchen and cook Sunday lunch for just the family.

'Should we invite Andy to join us?' asked Hugo.

'No, I want it to be just us. There'll be other times.'

Mid-afternoon, the phone rang and Maddy answered.

'Maddy! Does this mean Jamie's

home?' asked Guy.

'Not yet, but I'm having a day off.'

'I hope the place wasn't in too much of a state . . . '

'It was. Do you mean you knew?'

'I did, but what could I do? I suppose Val and Reg served some purpose being there?'

'Not a lot as it turns out. They'll be getting their marching orders when I see them.'

'How's Hugo? They'd been knocking it back when I got home. I'm sorry. Is he okay?'

'Nothing a bit of paracetamol won't cure, and it's hardly your fault.'

'And how are you, Maddy?'

'Relieved they've all survived. Furious at the state of the place. Val used to leave my old home immaculate. I can't understand what's happened.'

'I think you'll find Reg happened. He's an out-and-out slob.'

'That's what Hugo said. Well, I'll soon put it to rights. The twins have been a great help already. Oh, and

Andy's attacking the garden with great enthusiasm.'

'Is he now?'

Maddy could just see Guy's expression tightening. She could hear it in his voice. 'It's all right, Guy.'

'I suppose so.'

'Anyway, I can't sort out anything right now. I'm going back to hospital this evening.'

'Can I see you before you go?'

'I don't think there's time, but you could drive me back, if you wouldn't mind.'

'It will be my pleasure.'

⋆ ⋆ ⋆

Jamie was in excellent spirits when they arrived.

'You're looking better,' said Guy.

'I'm feeling it. I had four of my friends round the bed this afternoon. Staff had to tell them to keep quiet from time to time but she let them all stay. She seems to think the next time I see them I'll probably be home.'

'That is good news,' said Maddy.

'End of the week,' said the staff nurse, bustling in. 'That's if he behaves himself.'

Jamie grinned his old childish grin. 'I shall, staff.'

'I've made you some cookies,' said Maddy. 'You can share them with the nurses, or patients, whatever.'

When it was time for Guy to leave, Maddy walked with him to the outer door. 'Thanks for driving me in, Guy.'

'Come here,' he said, wrapping his arms round her and holding her close. 'This feels so right.'

'Mm,' she agreed. It felt like coming home.

'I'll see you soon.'

Without so much as a kiss he released her and left, but left her feeling cared for and loved. She'd never felt like that with Rob — well, certainly not for many years.

13

Guy walked into the ward mid-week, smartly dressed and cheerful. 'I'm taking your mother out for lunch. Is that all right with you, Jamie?'

'Sure,' he replied absently. 'I've got plenty to do. My friends thought my brain may be rotting so they brought me in lots of Sudoku and crosswords to keep me occupied.'

'See you later, then. Have fun.'

'You, too.'

'You heard that,' Guy murmured as they drove off. 'We've been instructed to have fun.'

She smiled. With Jamie on the mend she felt more like having fun than she had in a long time.

* * *

'You know all the best places,' Maddy

said as, having parked the car, they abandoned the chilly November air for the warmth of a bar with a beamed ceiling and a roaring fire in a vast fireplace.

He led her through to the cosy restaurant and chose a table by the window that looked out onto a lawn sloping down to a stream. 'What do you fancy? Pheasant, lasagne, or some locally caught fish?'

'How local?'

'Well, in a manner of speaking. We're not that far from the coast.'

She laughed and studied the menu. 'I fancy bream with chips and salad.'

'An eclectic choice.' The waiter appeared at that moment. 'Okay. Bream for the lady with chips and salad, and I'll have liver and bacon with extra vegetables.'

'Yes, sir. Anything to drink?'

'Maddy?'

'I'd like a glass of Pinot Grigio.'

'And I'll have Rioja. And we'll have a bottle of water. Still or sparkling, Maddy?'

'Sparkling, if that's all right for you.'

'Perfect.'

The food appeared in record time, or maybe they hadn't noticed time passing.

'This looks wonderful, Guy. So does yours. It's ages since I had liver and bacon in a pub.'

For reply he cut a sliver of tender liver, added a bit of bacon and offered her a forkful.

'Mm, nice.'

It was such a clichéd action but as she accepted the food, looking into his eyes, she experienced sensations which had nothing to do with the food.

They ate in silence for a while, then Guy put down his knife and fork.

'Maddy, I hope you don't mind me asking but do you still want to take the shop in Dorchester, now that Jamie's on the mend?'

'Ah.' She, too, laid down her cutlery. 'Decision time. I've thought about it endlessly in the wee small hours. The family will always be my number-one

348

concern as long as they need me but, with Liz's generous offer of help in setting it up, I think I can still make a go of Cupcakes and Candlesticks. I may have to learn to delegate more, though.'

'I think it will be wonderful. I can just picture it with dark red walls — or was it green?'

'I hadn't decided but I've had plenty of time to think. It's definitely going to be the dark antique red.'

'Good choice — and with spotlights it will be light enough, I'm sure.'

'And mirrors.'

'And mirrors, of course. I gather from Hugo that that agent for the units has been phoning.'

'Oh God, I should have let him know that's a definite no-no.'

'I'll ring him and let him know.'

'Thanks, Guy.'

'Do you fancy a pudding?'

Maddy looked through the menu. 'Ooh, don't they sound scrumptious. Sticky toffee pudding, chocolate fudge cake. I think I could manage a raspberry sorbet.'

'Coward.' He summoned the waiter, who had been preparing a table across the room. 'Two raspberry sorbets, please.'

'Certainly, sir.'

Guy seemed lost in thought on the drive back to the hospital and didn't linger once they got there. Maddy wondered if he was having second thoughts about their relationship. Perhaps he wanted to let her down gently. She and her family had certainly taken up a lot of his time since they had become neighbours. Well, it would have been too good to be true.

'Where's Guy?' Jamie asked as she walked in alone.

'He had things to do.'

'Oh. That's a shame. I like Guy. I wish I had a father like him.'

This was a surprise to Maddy. Jamie had always been so in awe of his own father. Now he'd discovered his hero had feet of clay. But was there a future for her and Guy?

On Friday Jamie was officially discharged, with instructions to rest as much as possible. Guy arrived with Hugo to take him and Maddy home.

'Where are we going?' Maddy asked.

'We thought you'd like to take another look at the shop, and Jamie hasn't seen it at all yet.'

'Cool,' said Jamie.

'I'll echo that,' said Maddy.

'Here we are then,' said Guy.

The four of them trouped in and Maddy stopped suddenly, gasping in astonishment. 'I don't believe it!'

'I think it's lovely,' said Jamie, puzzled.

'You don't understand, Jamie. When we came to see it, it was quite frankly a mess. Now look at it — all cleared up, walls painted the antique red I wanted, spotlights in the ceiling. Who's responsible?' She looked round accusingly at Guy and Hugo, who were quietly laughing, then not so quietly, and then

351

all four of them were laughing together.

'Guilty as charged,' Guy admitted. 'No, we actually got a firm of electricians and decorators in, and Hugo, Dom and I got a skip . . . '

'Two skips,' Hugo corrected.

'All right, two skips, and cleared the rubbish. Is it okay?'

'You know it is. It's perfect.'

'While the electrician was here we got him to install plenty of sockets every-where, including what I think you decided would be the kitchen area for the café upstairs.'

'I'm speechless.'

'Not like you, Mum,' said Jamie.

'I love it,' she said, hugging each of them in turn.

'I think we'd better get this young man home,' said Guy. 'You're beginning to look tired, Jamie.'

'I am a bit, but I can't wait to be reunited with Charlie.'

'Home we go then.'

* * *

Guy dropped them off and went home. The four children all congregated in the kitchen, lounging around with hot drinks and cookies.

'It's so good to be home,' Jamie said with a suppressed yawn.

'Save your energy for tomorrow night,' Dawn told him.

'What's happening then?'

'Guy's giving a welcome-home party for you at the manor and Robin's having his fireworks party on Monday.'

'That's nice,' said Jamie. 'I shan't be dancing on the tables, though.'

'Oh come here.' Dawn gave him a bear hug. 'It's so good to have you home, little bro.'

'It's good to be home,' he repeated, extricating himself.

'Likewise,' Sophie declared, hugging him rather more gently. 'You're not saying ouch. That's good.'

'Should be good grub tomorrow night,' said Hugo. 'Mrs F's best.'

'I like Mrs F's cooking,' said Jamie. 'It's kind of Dorset country food.'

'We all like it, too,' the twins assured him.

'Where's Charlie?' asked Jamie.

'Oh don't worry, squirt. Dom's taken him and his brother Sam for a short walk. He'll be bringing him back soon.'

'I want to take him for walks. Surely I can do that.'

'You sure can, only not for a few days. We promised the doctors you would do a lot of resting for a while, and Charlie has a lot to learn about behaving on the end of a leash. Wait till Dr Phillips visits and signs you off.'

'When's that going to be?'

'Soon, I think,' Maddy told him. 'He's coming to see you on Monday. Oh look, Andy's arrived to do some gardening. Why don't you go and chat to him? Do you good to get a spot of sunshine, well wrapped up of course.'

'Of course,' Jamie echoed wryly. 'God, you're all treating me like a baby.'

'We're all grateful you're still around. I've never seen anyone look so ill, and survive.'

'What's he doing here so early, anyway? I'm not doing lessons yet.'

'It's his half-day off. He spends his spare time working on our garden — for fun, he says. He wants to talk to you about doing some work in the holidays so that you're not too far behind when you go back to school.'

'There are other subjects besides maths.'

'Precisely! He wants to talk about that, too. I believe he has some notes for you from your other teachers.'

Jamie groaned. 'I'd better go and see what mental torture he's planned. Some Christmas this is going to be.'

Sophie held his padded jacket while he put it on, tied a scarf round his neck and handed him some gloves. They then watched him through the window walk slowly over to where Andy was working. After a short exchange, Andy fetched a garden chair and gestured for Jamie to sit down. He stood leaning on a spade while he and Jamie talked. From Jamie's gestures of mock despair they could guess how the conversation was going.

'I'm going to take them some tea,' Dawn declared.

'Nosy cow!' Sophie said with a laugh. Nevertheless she followed her twin, carrying a jar of cookies.

'It's nice to see the girls looking after their brother,' said Maddy, walking into the kitchen.

'Isn't it just?' Hugo replied drily. 'Nothing to do with the fact that it's Andy he's talking to. What have you been up to, Mum?'

'I've been making some phone calls, answering queries for dinner parties, and I've got orders for a dozen or so cakes, too. I think there's rather more than I can handle. I might have to hire some help for the festive season. I can do cakes here but I don't want to spend all my time in other people's houses, now I've got the family together again. I can't leave Jamie on his own — not for a while. Fortunately, there are always catering

356

students hungry for experience.'

'Mum, Jamie's a lot better. We'll all look after him. He's still weak but he's not going to go back to the worst days of his illness — the doctors said so.'

'I know that logically, but I can't help but worry.'

'You never used to be a worrier. I'm really sorry for all the trouble we've caused you.'

'Jamie's illness wasn't deliberate.'

'No, but Dawn's drug-taking episode and my drinking were purely self-induced.'

'You're young, and the young make mistakes.'

'So do the old — like Dad.'

'Talking of whom — I had a letter from the solicitor yesterday reminding me to go in and sign for the decree absolute. I expect there'll be a hefty bill from him, too.'

'What's the significance of the decree absolute?'

'It ends the marriage legally and leaves your father and me free of each other.'

'And he'll be free to marry that woman, if he wants to.'

'He will,' Maddy replied thoughtfully, surprised to find the thought not in the least upsetting.

That evening they sat round and enjoyed chicken casserole and gooseberry fool. Andy joined them since it was a Friday.

'I haven't really earned my supper today,' he joked.

'I'd say you have — more than,' Maddy replied, 'with all the work you're putting into the garden.'

'I enjoy it, and I thought it might earn me some brownie points. I don't want to seem pushy, but have you decided if and when I can move into the flat?'

'I have, and you can move in as soon as you like.'

'Wonderful. I'm between books, as it were, at the moment, although a bunch of characters are queuing up in my mind, demanding that I write their story.'

'That sounds interesting.'

'We've had a talk, Jamie and I, about the tuition — haven't we, Jamie? — and as soon as he's ready, most likely after Christmas, we'll start lessons again. In the meantime I've got a load of bumpf from other teachers for him to peruse.'

'Lucky me,' said Jamie mournfully, and everyone laughed.

'You can feed Charlie after supper if you like, and take him round the orchard, if you're up to it.'

'Of course I am.'

Andy left early to have a Christmas drink with some members of staff, at one of their homes. After he'd gone, they all sat round playing board games, all seemingly wanting to be together on Jamie's first night home.

The next morning, Maddy woke before six and decided to take advantage of the hour to make a start on customers' orders for Christmas cakes. By ten o'clock, when the children started to appear, she had six in the ovens well on the way to being cooked.

'Wow! They smell good,' said Hugo, the first down.

'Yes, baking large quantities is easy with the equipment I've bought. Icing them is much more time-consuming. I've got another six to make, but for now I've run out of ingredients. I'll need to go shopping later. Do you think I should make a pudding or something to take over to Guy's tonight?'

'No, certainly not without talking to Mrs F first. You don't want to insult her.'

'How right you are, and how thoughtful, Hugo. We'll just take some wine then, shall we, and maybe some cheese.'

'I'm sure she won't object to that.'

Having no big evening meal to prepare that day, Maddy went into town and bought the ingredients she needed for the other cakes. She also bought ground almonds for the marzipan and ingredients for the royal icing.

Back home, as she measured and mixed, she realised she loved cooking

— but mainly for people she loved or at least knew. When she took on the shop she would employ staff to run it when she couldn't be there. No more Wonder Woman.

★   ★   ★

The children took Charlie out for a walk before lunch. Alone in the house, Maddy heard a strange noise coming from the study. She hurried there and saw that the Skype phone was ringing and flashing its rich blue light. She picked it up.

'Hello?'

'Maddy? Is that you?'

Rob! 'Yes, Rob, it's me. You've just missed the children, I'm afraid. They've taken Charlie for a walk.'

'Who's Charlie?'

'The new puppy. Didn't they mention him? He's a gorgeous yellow Labrador.'

'Dogs aren't gorgeous. You've become a regular load of country bumpkins, haven't you?'

'Have we? What did you want, Rob?'

'Well, I don't want to quarrel with you, Maddy. Look darling, Holly and I have split up. I'm at the airport now with a ticket to the UK. I thought we — that is, you and I — could try again. I know I've been a naughty boy and it won't be easy . . . '

'Just like that? I'm absolutely speechless!'

'Not like you, Mads.'

She felt a red mist rising in front of her. 'What about your child?'

'Holly's child, you mean. She confessed it was someone else's, not mine, or Simon's, but she tricked me into thinking it was mine because she thought I'd make a good provider.'

'She said that?'

'I could read between the lines. Maddy, you and I have got so much going for us, four wonderful children; and now you've moved away from Bournemouth, we can make a fresh start. I'm sure I'll love the country and I might even grow to love

362

— Charlie, was it?'

She wasn't listening. She was trying to imagine Rob moving in with them, everyone pussyfooting around him and his moods, shrugging off his constant criticism and putdowns. It was impossible. She couldn't do it.

'Rob, you're a million miles away from me — geographically, emotionally, every which way. There's no way I could ever get back with you. Once we have the decree absolute, we both need to move on.' Nor did she intend to upset the children who had become used to their new life without Rob.

'But Holly has taken practically everything and ploughed it into her family business. I've got hardly anything to move on with.'

'Well, that's between you and her, Rob.' Maddy hardened her heart, as she realised the true reason for him wanting to come back. 'Sue her if you have to. You and I are well and truly over — you'd just better believe it.'

'Your father called while you were out,' she told the children as they trouped in with a wet and muddy Charlie. 'There's a towel over there to dry Charlie.'

'What did he want?' asked Sophie.

'He said he and Holly have split up — a matter of the baby not being his, but she's apparently taken him for practically every penny. He thought he could move back in with us and we could make a fresh start.'

'My heart bleeds,' said Dawn. 'I hope you said no. He was always so bad-tempered. He didn't like us.'

'He didn't even want to know when Jamie was in hospital,' Sophie added. 'You did say no, didn't you?'

'I did, actually.'

'I'm glad,' Jamie declared, which was a huge relief. 'I don't mind seeing him occasionally if he comes back to the UK, but I don't want to live with him again.'

'How about you, Hugo?'

364

'Need I spell it out? I may forgive him one day, but right now I'm still angry with him. No, I don't want him around.'

Maddy breathed a sigh of relief.

14

They arrived at the manor at seven, pulled the old-fashioned bell and walked in. Guy was just crossing the hall.

'Come in. Welcome, all of you. Everyone's in the drawing room.' He could never bring himself to call the large, elegant room a sitting room. That was reserved for a cosier room of lesser proportions.

'Shall we take these to the kitchen, Guy?' she asked, indicating the cheeses and wine she and Hugo were carrying.

'Yes, please. Here, let me give you a hand.' He took her package from her, and Hugo followed him to the kitchen so she and Guy didn't have a moment alone.

'Do put your coats in the cloakroom,' said Guy.

Maddy listened to the murmur of

conversation and laughter coming from the drawing room. Clearly Guy had other guests, which she hadn't expected for some reason. They entered the room all together and the first person Maddy spotted was Liz, her sister-in-law.

'Hello, Liz. This is a surprise,' she said. 'What are you doing here?'

'I was surprised to be invited myself, but I wasn't going to turn down the chance of a good party and, hopefully, a decent meal. Oh, and meet David. The invitation said 'and friend' so I brought him. He's a partner in the firm.'

David was tall and well-preserved — late fifties, Maddy guessed; and, from the way they looked at each other, rather more than a colleague. Good for Liz.

'Nice to meet you, David.'

'Likewise.' He had a charming smile and good teeth, she noted inconsequentially. 'I've heard quite a lot about you. How's your young son? Jamie, is it?'

'See for yourself.'

There followed a round of introductions. Guy managed to lead Maddy away to where Dominic was chatting to Robin and his parents.

'You know Robin, and these are his parents, Edward and Maria.'

'Actually we've met,' said Maria with a smile. 'Maddy cooked us a delicious supper last time we were down for the weekend.'

'I see. Your reputation's spreading far and wide, Maddy.'

'Oh before I forget,' said Robin, 'we're having a bonfire party at the vicarage on Monday. I hope you and your family will all come.'

'Thanks. I'm sure we'd all love to.'

'In that case, can I borrow the boys to help build the bonfire tomorrow?'

'Okay, boys?'

Hugo and Jamie exchanged a nod. 'We'll be there,' said Hugo.

'I'll make sure he doesn't overdo it.'

'Thanks, Robin.'

Mrs Frimley appeared at the door. 'It's all ready, Guy,' she told him.

'Excellent, Mrs. F. Thank you. Shall we go in, everyone?'

They all trouped into the dining room to find a beautifully laid table graced with the best family silver and crystal.

'It looks wonderful, Guy!' Maddy exclaimed. 'Mrs Frimley's excelled herself this time.'

'Hasn't she just?'

The lady in question wheeled in a trolley in the wake of the guests. They were walking slowly round the table, taking their places according to little name cards which Maddy guessed Dominic had produced on his computer. She was pleased to find herself seated to Guy's right, while Robin's mother sat on his left. Her other neighbour was Robin.

'I'll be off now, Guy,' said Mrs Frimley, 'if that's all right.'

'Thank you, Mrs F. You've done us proud. Oh, this is for you — a little extra towards a Christmas shopping spree.' He handed her an envelope which, if its thickness was anything to go by, contained more than a little extra.

'That's very kind of you, Guy. Shall I come in tomorrow?'

'No, thank you. You've earned your weekend off.'

'See you Monday, then.'

Guy proceeded to carve the joints of beef and turkey which were on the trolley, while dishes of vegetables and accompaniments were set around the table. When everyone had been served with meat, the dishes were passed around.

They were all feeling mellow by the time they reached the pudding stage. Hugo kept to sensible limits with the wine, as did the girls, and Maddy was pleased to see that they had now moved on to mineral water. Jamie had no desire to drink anything else. Robin and his parents had become quite expansive, as had Liz and David, but she noted that Guy was hardly touching his wine.

'Are you all right?' she asked quietly.

'I'm more than all right, Maddy. I'm pleasantly content to be surrounded by my favourite people.'

Maddy smiled, her eyes unknowingly full of love. She was wearing the lovely bracelet he had given her, which made her smile just to look at it. The twins had enthused about it when they saw it but did not seem particularly surprised that Guy should give her such a present.

'I could say the same, but I'm particularly delighted to have all my family together again.'

'You don't find it strange saying 'all my family' when it used to include two parents?'

'Not at all, and all links will shortly be severed with Rob when I get the decree absolute.'

'No kidding! What a lovely early Christmas present — or is it?' He looked searchingly into her eyes.

'It is,' she said firmly.

'Puddings!' he announced, seeing

that everyone had stopped eating.

Maddy and the twins piled all the used dishes onto the trolley and wheeled it out. Hugo and Dominic emptied it in the kitchen, setting one load going in the dishwasher and stacking the rest to make up the next load. After wiping down the trolley it was recharged with Dorset apple cake, fruit salad, cream and the cheese board, which contained Guy's choice of cheddar and Dorset Blue Vinny and Maddy's selection of continental cheeses, colourfully garnished with black and green grapes. They were enjoying the last few crumbs on their plates when Guy rose to his feet and tapped his glass.

'I'd like to start by saying how delighted I am that you were all able to come this evening. We're particularly delighted to see Jamie back with his family.' Maddy noted that Jamie looked a trifle pale — understandably, in spite of the rest he had had after lunch. 'It's been a year of change for Maddy and her family, and a time of growing happiness for Dom and me, having such delightful neighbours. Now, I'm going to do something unforgivable and put Maddy on the spot.'

Maddy looked at him with alarm. What on earth was he going to say?

'I've thought long and hard before interfering but I've discussed this with Liz, Maddy's former sister-in-law.' That little 'former' did not go unnoticed. 'Liz and I thought you may not be so keen, Maddy, in view of current events — namely Jamie's illness — to set up a new, time-consuming business in the Dorchester shop right now. Later, maybe. You have a nice little earner with your special cakes and the occasional dinner party.'

Maddy was starting to feel annoyed. She wanted to tell Guy her thoughts on the matter herself. She wanted to tell him about her plans for Cupcakes and Candlesticks. How dare they discuss how she should run her life — even if there was a grain of truth in what he was saying.

'If you were to run cookery courses as well, you would have plenty to do and still be there for the children . . . '

'Oh, but . . . '

She'd had similar thoughts, but what was it to do with Guy?

'Another alternative . . . ' He seemed to be finding it difficult to go on. 'An alternative which seems to me to be the best option, would be . . . ' His voice dropped almost to a whisper. ' . . . for you to marry me, Maddy; move into the manor and do whatever else you want to do.'

He stopped talking and there was a stunned silence as his words sank in, followed by gasps and exclamations of delight. Maddy studied the faces of her four children. To her astonishment, they all looked pleased. Hugo started to clap, followed by Dominic, and everyone started talking at once.

Overwhelmed, Maddy stood up and wandered out to the peace and quiet of the study. Guy followed. She turned on him.

'You've got it all worked out, haven't you?' she said with a touch of asperity.

'No, of course I haven't.' He stood beside the fireplace, leaning on the mantelpiece, while Maddy stood across the room. 'I'm sorry if I embarrassed you in front of my guests and your family, but I love you and I want the whole world to know it. I don't want a hole-in-the-corner affair, as I've said before. I talked to Liz to get her perspective and, frankly, to get her on side. She doesn't have a lot of respect for her brother, I gather. You've been running yourself ragged lately with all your problems. You've faced them all alone and with great courage. I don't want you to be alone, though. I thought, wrongly it seems, that you cared for me as I care for you . . . '

'I do, Guy.' She crossed the room. 'I do care for you. I realised just how much this afternoon when Rob phoned. He's split up with his lady love and wants to come back to the UK. He suggested we could start again but I told him it was impossible. I couldn't imagine it. I didn't tell him, but it's you I love. I couldn't contemplate living with Rob again. Fortunately, the children feel the same. I would be delighted to spend my life with you — but I still intend to run Cupcakes and Candlesticks! You shouldn't have sprung your proposal on me like that.'

'I think I should,' he said softly. 'This way, we don't have to tell everyone individually. Even Robin approves.'

'But what about my house — well, the one I'm living in?' She pressed a finger to his lips. 'And please don't say 'details'.'

'Well, what else?' He grinned. 'Presuming we're all going to live here, it would make a stunning holiday let; or, if you want to run catering courses, accommodation for students. The possibilities are endless. There's nothing we can't overcome if we love each other and pull together.'

'But I've promised the flat to Andy.'

'Oh, Andy!' He gave her a severe look. 'I know you've got a soft spot for Andy, but he's a single man. He can easily find somewhere else to live.'

'Poor Andy. He rather liked the prospect of living there, doing a bit of gardening . . . '

'Being close to you?'

'Don't be silly.'

'He can still live in the flat, whatever we do with the house. It's self-contained, after all.'

'I suppose so.'

She had somehow moved into Guy's arms and settled against him, wondering how it would feel to be free to hold him and love him, have his company by day and his loving by night.

'Do you think the children really do approve?' she wondered aloud.

'I'm sure they do. No one seemed shocked. Surprised, maybe. As to Dominic, he adores you and your family. He and Hugo are talking digs-sharing next year at uni. They both want to do law and Hugo doesn't want a gap year to travel like the one Dom had planned. So if Hugo gets in, and I gather he's expected to, they'll certainly be happy. What about the twins and Jamie?'

Maddy remembered Dawn's comment about their visit to the unit. 'Guy's little woman — cool!' And she related the incident to Guy.

'Would Jamie also think it cool?' he asked.

'He looked pleased enough to me just now and he did say the other day he wished he had a father like you.'

'Did he, now? I'm flattered. So, Maddy Leighton, how do feel about becoming Maddy Deverill?' He slid effortlessly to one knee and asked, seriously and lovingly: 'Maddy, my darling wonderful Maddy, will you do me the honour of becoming my wife?'

'Oh Guy, I'd love to marry you.'

They returned to the dining room with their arms around each other.

'Well,' said Liz, 'I don't think we need to ask your decision, Maddy. We're all delighted for you both, aren't we, folks.'

As they were congratulated by one and all, Dominic excused himself and returned carrying bottles of champagne, obviously chilled in readiness.

'Are you sure it's what you want, Mum?' asked Hugo, handing her a slender crystal flute of the sparkling liquid.

'I'm quite sure, for myself. What about you, Hugo? Is it all right with you and the others?'

'We're all over the moon for you.'

'Dear Hugo. You've been my rock these last few months. I'll always remember that.' She took a sip of champagne and set her glass down. 'Come here.' She gave him a hug and the next moment the twins and Jamie joined in for a family hug, laughing somewhat tearfully.

'Can anyone join in?' asked Dominic, and soon found himself enclosed in an enlarged family hug.

'My turn, I think,' said Guy, 'but I want Maddy all to myself.'

After which he and Maddy circulated among the other guests, accepting their good wishes for a happy future, of which Maddy had no doubt.

15

A time of frantic preparation for Christmas ensued. There were cards to write, presents to buy and wrap, orders to complete. In the midst of it all, Andy dropped in one morning while the children were at the manor helping to erect and decorate a large Christmas tree in the hall.

'Andy! Come in.'

'Hello, Maddy,' he said quietly. 'I gather congratulations are in order.'

'Thank you, Andy. I'm glad you called. We've been talking about what to do with this house. We have various ideas, but whatever we decide, if you still want the flat it's yours.'

'Actually I've had a change of plan. I've received an absolutely indecent advance for my book and I've found a cottage near my parents in Worcestershire, which will be quiet and perfect for writing. I'm moving there.'

'Well, congratulations, Andy. I'm really happy for you.'

'And I for you, I guess. Guy's a lucky man. It's been great knowing you, Maddy. Oh, I almost forgot. Here's a Christmas card, and a copy from the first run of my novel.'

With which he turned on his heel and left. Maddy watched him go, wondering. She opened the envelope he had given her and was just reading the card inside when Guy pulled up in the drive and wandered in.

'Early card, sweetheart?'

'Not the first,' she replied, lifting her face for his kiss. 'It's from Andy, and that's a copy of his first novel.'

Guy slid the book out of the see-through packet and opened it.

'I see. Should I be jealous?'

'What are you talking about?' Maddy took the book from him and read the words: 'To a special lady. I guess the better man won. Love from Andy,' followed by a row of kisses.

She looked up at the 'better man'.

'I'd no idea. Poor Andy.' She couldn't spend too long feeling sorry for Andy, though. He was a lovely young man — well, younger than her, anyway. He would soon find himself a more suitable love, of that she was sure. She grinned up at Guy. 'You can be jealous if you like.'

'Why would I be? I've got everything I could ever wish for. I came over actually to invite you to join us for a simple lunch of soup followed by mince pies.'

'Lovely. I'll fetch my coat.'

'No hurry. Do you realise we've got the place to ourselves? Come here.'

She slid into his arms and it was quite a while before she fetched that coat.

THE END

THE SECRET OF THE SILVER LOCKET

Jill Barry

Orphan Grace Walker will come of age in 1925, having spent years as companion to the daughter of an aristocratic family. Grace believes her origins are humble, but as her birthday approaches, an encounter with young American professor Harry Gresham offers the chance of love and a new life. What could possibly prevent her from seizing happiness? A silver locket holds a vital clue, and a letter left by Grace's late mother reveals shocking news. Only Harry can piece the puzzle together . . .